Give the Gift of Knowledge

The Perpetual Book Fund

This book was
generously donated
by
Ms. Mary McCabe
in memory of
Dawn Jonas

November 2010

My Invisible Sister

MY INVISIBLE SISTER

Beatrice Colin and Sara Pinto

BLOOMSBURY

NEW YORK BERLIN LONDON

Published by Bloomsbury Books for Young Readers
175 Fifth Avenue, New York, New York 10010

Library of Congress Cataloging-in-Publication Data
Colin, Beatrice.
My invisible sister / by Beatrice Colin & Sara Pinto. — 1st U.S. ed.
          p.   cm.
Summary: Ten-year-old Frank's thirteen-year-old sister Elizabeth, invisible since birth,
continually causes trouble, forcing the family to move again and again, but Frank
wants to stay put and decides to find a way to make her visible.
ISBN 978-1-59990-488-7
[1. Brothers and sisters—Fiction. 2. Moving, Household—Fiction. 3. Conduct of life—
Fiction. 4. Neighbors—Fiction. 5. Schools—Fiction. 6. Family life—Fiction. 7. Science
fiction.] I. Pinto, Sara. II. Title.
PZ7.C677477My 2010   [Fic]—dc22   2009032631

First U.S. Edition June 2010
Book design by Nicole Gastonguay
Typeset by Westchester Book Composition
Printed in the U.S.A. by Worldcolor Fairfield, Pennsylvania
2 4 6 8 10 9 7 5 3 1

For Aidan, Lucca, Cecilia, and William—
and all their invisible friends
—S. P.

For my children, Theo and Frances
—B. C.

MY
INVISIBLE
SISTER

Chapter One

"Frank!" shouts my sister, Elizabeth. "Are you going to sit in there all day?"

It's another fine day in suburbia. Every flower is in bloom, every car is polished, every lawn is a perfect square of green. A pack of little kids plays on their bikes. The local ice-cream truck jingles past, playing "Somewhere Over the Rainbow."

The only thing spoiling the view is the van—our gigantic moving van with "Jerry's Budget Budge-It" pasted on the side. Our whole life is wrapped up and boxed inside, just waiting to be unpacked. I climb out of the van and pick up a box at random.

"Not that one," says Dad. It's the only remaining box of Mom's best china.

"I can handle it," I say.

"Just don't drop it," he warns me.

I stand back and look up at our new house. It's the same as all the other houses in the neighborhood. Red brick, white front door, and two-car garage. The only thing that stands out is a huge tree in the backyard.

"What do you think?" Dad asks. "There's space in the garage for all your gear, your bike, and your skateboard. And the yard's big enough to play ball with Bob."

Bob is my dog. He barks twice every time you say his name. He runs up to my dad and, guess what, barks twice.

"It seems good," I say.

"Great," Dad says. "Now let's get to work."

As I walk up the front path with the box in my arms, I notice a kid about my age. He's sitting on a bike in the yard next door. I have to say, he looks kind of cool. I'm about to say hi but instead I go, "Arr-ghhphft!" Something has clamped me in the armpits. I stumble, barely hanging on to the box; regain my balance; and am immediately tripped. I stagger toward the flower bed but, just before I reach it, I'm propelled back onto the sidewalk. Miraculously, I manage to hang on to the box.

"Careful, you nearly dropped it," a voice whispers in my ear.

"Are you okay?" asks the cool guy.

"What is wrong with you?" I say.

"Nothing," says the cool guy.

"You moron!" I yell.

The box is wrenched from my grip, hovers in midair for a moment, and then falls to the ground, making all the sounds that a box of your mother's best china would make if it were breaking into a million pieces.

"Oh, Frank," moans my mom. "You dropped the box!"

"It wasn't me!" I reply.

And really, it wasn't.

You might think I am one of those boys who has everything: a bike, a skateboard (customized, of course), a dog named Bob, and a new house. But it's what you *can't* see that ruins everything.

I have a sister. "So what?" you might say. "I've got one or two or six myself." Well, I would take your six and give you my skateboard, my bike, and even my dog if you'd take my sister.

In many ways, Elizabeth is just like any other

thirteen-year-old girl. She likes music, clothes, and talking on the phone. The one thing that sets her apart is her looks. She doesn't have any. When my sister was born, the doctor almost dropped her. She was eight pounds exactly, she had a full set of lungs, and she screamed until the place shook, but she was one hundred percent invisible. I'm not joking. Her condition, known as *Formus Disappearus*, is a rare and untreatable genetic disease. Although you may not have heard of it, there have been dozens of people with this problem throughout history—like the Tooth Fairy (real name Annie Morrison). For reasons I'll never understand, she collected millions of teeth and started a craze.

As long as I can remember, my sister's been mean to me. She teases me, she trips me, she frames me, she blames me, she needles me, and when I try to get her back, she's never there. Or anywhere. Punching the air, grabbing on to nothing, or lashing out at shadows just makes me look crazy. My parents tell me it's not her fault, that I should be more understanding—but they should try being her brother. And when she's unhappy, the only thing they can come up with is "a fresh start."

This is our eighth move in ten years. "Can you

4

believe it?" I ask Bob. "*You* do the math." He lets out a tiny growl and starts to wag his tail. No, he can't believe it either (or do the math). Every time we move, my parents promise better things. Better friends, better schools, better everything. Enter Elizabeth. Exit new life. Wonder how long we'll last in this place?

The cool boy next door is staring at me, looking puzzled and insulted at the same time—he thinks I just called him a moron. I decide to use the pretend-nothing-happened tactic.

"Hi, I'm Frank," I say.

He just stares at me—at the top of my head, actually.

"And this is my sister, Elizabeth. Elizabeth, say hi."

She says nothing. Typical. I can see his mind working. He stares harder and takes half a step backward. He thinks I'm a nut.

Dad walks up the path, a stack of boxes in his arms, and almost trips over Mom's broken china.

"Tell me you didn't."

"I didn't!" I reply.

Dad shakes his head; he's not listening. As usual, it's my fault. I pick up the box and we both lug our loads toward the new house.

"I'd like to welcome you all to 44 Morningvale

Circle," says Dad, "our new home. Have you kids seen the backyard?"

"I hate that big tree," Elizabeth says. "It blocks out all the sun. The backyard is Shade Central."

"She does have a point," Mom says.

"We can always take it down," Dad says, already sounding tired.

"I like it," I interject. "No one else has a tree that size. We could build a tree house."

"Oh great," says my sister.

"Elizabeth," says Dad, "just give it a try. I'm sure once we settle in, we'll never want to leave. Elizabeth?"

"She's gone, Dad."

This is how it always starts. Each time we move, we leave behind angry neighbors, broken friendships, and piles of junk mail. There's always a reason. House too small, school too big, town too far away, neighbors too close, road too busy, lawn dead. My parents don't want to see that the real problem is usually sitting in the living room, reading gossip magazines and drinking the last of the milk.

It's only when we put down our boxes that my dad says casually, "You may want to think twice about wearing underwear on your head. It makes a kind of goofy first impression."

"Elizabeth!" I yell. "Not again! You made me look like a total jerk!"

"Keep your shirt on," she says. "We'll probably be out of here by Christmas."

Normally, I would freak out. Normally, I would go tearing around the house punching frantically, hoping for contact and screaming her name. But this time, I don't. It comes to me in a great big thunder-and-lightning, eureka-moment kind of way. If I still want to be here past Christmas, then I have to take matters into my own hands. I've got to keep a handle on Elizabeth. Because I'm not moving again. I'm tired of it—tired of not living in a place long enough to make any friends and tired of always being the new boy in town. This is the house I want to grow up in. This is where I want to stay. And Bob is in total agreement. He usually is.

It's almost eight o'clock when Bob and I go for a walk around the block. I can hear the sound of the neighbors' television sets all tuned to the same channel. Our TV is lost again. Buried under some pile, probably. Dad's gone to take the moving van back and to pick up the customary first-night Chinese takeout.

The kid next door is working on his bike.

"Hey there," I say, acting casual.

He nods but doesn't answer.

"Fixing your bike?"

He looks at me with an expression that says, "What's it look like, duh?"

Clearly the damage has already been done.

"See you later," I call. He doesn't answer.

Bob and I decide to go exploring. There are five houses in this cul-de-sac, all set around a large tear-shaped piece of concrete. Beyond that, there's not much to see—just endless houses all set into circles like ours. It would be easy to get lost in a place like this: nothing changes but the color of people's cars.

Five minutes later we're back again. The kid is still pumping his tires. He's out of breath and his face is bright red. Either he's got inner-tube problems or he's more of a wimp than he looks. But, wait a minute, I remember that the same thing happened to me last year. As fast as he pumps one tire, the other goes flat. It's a typical Elizabeth stunt.

With perfect timing, Dad appears with the Chinese food. "Dinner's here," he shouts. My sister won't hang around now. She's a sucker for chicken chop suey.

"It's your inner trig pressure," I say nonchalantly.

"I don't think it has anything to do with trigs, whatever they are."

"Let me try. I think I can fix that for you."

I pump the tires and, without Elizabeth's sabotaging, they stay that way. The kid is impressed.

"It must have been the trig thing after all. Thanks."

"Frank and Bob," Mom calls, "your crispy duck is getting cold."

Bob barks twice and runs into the house. It's our favorite dish.

"I'm not really that hungry." I shrug.

"You like baseball cards?" says the kid next door.

"I *love* baseball cards," I reply. This, I am afraid, is a lie. I loathe and detest baseball with every fiber in my body. I'm more of a skateboarding guy.

"I've got four albums. Some of the cards are really, really rare."

"Cool," I say. "Can I see them?"

My new friend is named Charlie and he's ten, like me. And even though he likes baseball, he's pretty nice. Because he's an only child, he has shelves of neatly stacked toys and no one to play with. By the time I head inside my new house, I'm starving and tired—but it was all worth it. We've already planned our first project. We're going to build a tree house in my backyard. Elizabeth may be invisible, but hey, she's not invincible.

"I'm home," I yell as I close the front door.

"Bob and I ate your dinner," says my sister from the direction of the couch. "Oh, and aren't you going to thank me?"

"Thank *you*? For what?"

"Don't you know when you've been set up? You'd never have any friends if it weren't for me. . . . 'I *love* baseball cards. . . .'"

I ignore her. "We started the plans for the tree house. It's going to be awesome."

"No it's not. That tree's coming down. Dad promised me. And besides, you wouldn't even know how to build a birdhouse."

Out of habit, I pick the closest throwable object, a single rubber boot, and hurl it in her direction. From the sound it makes, I think it hits her.

"You are so going to pay for that." She gasps. "I'm going to get you when you least expect it."

Chapter Two

Now that you understand what I have to put up with in the sister department, let me tell you a little more about my parents. My father reviews restaurants for newspapers. This means lots of free dinners in fancy places where snotty waiters have to be nice to him. My mother is a party planner for rich people and minor celebrities. Apart from all the signed photographs of people neither I, nor probably you, have ever heard of, she's always bringing home leftovers, like trays of miniature hamburgers or boxes of chocolate-covered strawberries.

You may think that they sound awesome, eccentric, even cool, but I can tell you there have been many times when I wished I had the kind of parents who worked at normal boring jobs with normal boring hours.

Because my parents are always working, we've been here a week and have barely unpacked. You'd think that with all their moving experience, my parents would be experts at it by now. But they are actually getting worse. So far Dad has unpacked his vintage guitar collection, and it's taking up the entire living room. Mom's getting reacquainted with her designer shoes, which she thought she had lost five moves ago. Elizabeth has shut herself in her room and has obviously managed to unearth her entire CD collection. Nobody can find the silverware, the can opener, or the bath towels. There's a good chance we will never see those things again.

I've unpacked and my room is fully furnished with all my stuff. I've learned to mark my boxes. Simple but effective: "Clothing," "Action Figures," "Books," and, of course, "Miscellaneous." The mistake the rest of my family makes is that every box is "Miscellaneous." The toothpaste is thrown in with the cookbooks. Hamster food (Chippy died two years ago) is in with the defunct computer monitor and the spice rack. The bedding, we think, is being used to cushion the coffeemaker. And they wonder why they lose things.

Currently we are eating our dinner straight from the pan and drinking juice out of jam jars. I have to say that we're used to it by now, but it's not something any of us really want the neighbors to see.

I'm in my bedroom reenacting the fight scene at the end of *Star Wars: Revenge of the Sith* when I realize this is the seventh time I've heard Green Day's "American Idiot." It's not that it's a bad song, but enough is enough. First I try the polite approach. I knock on the door. No answer.

"Would you mind adjusting the volume?" I ask nicely.

The volume is cranked up.

"Don't wanna be . . . ," the CD blasts.

"Turn it down!" I yell.

Nothing.

"Turn it down, idiot head!"

The music stops. Elizabeth's door flies open.

"What did you call me?"

"I asked you politely and you ignored me. I was forced into a more, um, . . . direct approach."

She laughs in my face.

"You"—I feel a sharp poke in my chest—"are a freak. No, let me be more specific. You like to wear underpants on your head. Need I say more?"

I know I should ignore her and just walk away. But the underpants thing really gets me. I see red. My week-long efforts to not let her bug me, to not take the bait, to turn the other cheek, to swallow my pride, suddenly evaporate. Before I can stop myself, my right fist is clenched into a ball and I swing out. To my surprise, I make contact. It's hard to know exactly where the blow lands, but my guess is that it's a direct hit to the stomach. I regret it immediately.

"I'm so sorry, really . . . I didn't mean it."

"That's the second time you've done that!"

I feel her whiz past me.

"Elizabeth? . . . Please don't wreck it for us here!"

Downstairs, the front door slams.

This is a cul-de-sac where the mailman's visit is about as exciting as it gets. Then we move in, and almost immediately strange things will start to happen. It won't take long before everybody here hates us. Trust me, I've seen it happen many times.

So I'm out there, practically thirty seconds after Elizabeth, but she has the definite advantage. As you know, Charlie lives right next door. His mom works nights in the local maternity hospital. Next to him is some old man who lives by himself and constantly trims his hedges. To our left is a family with a ton of kids. From the outside it looks as if they are all five years old, but that can't be right. Next to them is a little old lady. Her yard is so full of cheery little gnomes, it's depressing.

To be honest, I've been expecting payback from Elizabeth ever since we arrived last week. So far, however, everything seems to be in order . . . birds are chirping, vacuum cleaners are gently humming, radios are forecasting cloudless skies. . . . It suddenly occurs to me that I could be overreacting. Maybe Elizabeth simply has gone for a walk, perhaps to cool off or to buy a small gift of apology.

Who am I kidding?

Above the sweet sounds of suburbia, I hear a loud knock. I'm guessing it came from next door to Charlie. I break out into a cold sweat. Oh, no—not the Bang and Bolt Routine. This is Elizabeth's favorite— banging on people's doors, ringing their bells, and when they open up, there's no one there. The neighbors will know it's us, the weird new family. And so I do the first thing that comes into my head. I run like crazy and reach Hedge Man's door, just as he opens it.

"Hi, Mr. Hedge, I mean, I mean . . ." Panting, I frantically scan the door for a name. He frowns at me. There's no name anywhere. "I mean, your hedge, it looks so good, so neat."

I turn around and gaze intently at his handiwork. It doesn't even look like something belonging to the plant family. He probably doesn't realize it, but it looks like a giant green LEGO piece plopped into his yard, complete with the raised things that you need to stick the pieces together.

A smile appears on his bad-tempered face.

"It's so refreshing to meet a youngster interested in topiary."

I look at him blankly.

"The art of trimming evergreen trees or shrubs into ornamental sculptures." He points to a bush in the shape of a bird perched on his lawn.

He looks over toward our house. Of course, our hedges, if you could call them that, are a mess.

"I'd be happy to offer a small demonstration, if you're interested."

Bang, bang! The door to the left of our house gets pounded on.

"I am," I say. "I am so . . . interested. Give me a holler when you'd like to do it."

I start to back off down the driveway.

"No time like the present," he says. "I'll expect you at five o'clock sharp. Today."

Luckily, the woman with all the kids is slow to answer her door. As I'm catching my breath, I can hear the sounds of several babies screaming their heads off. Not my scene. The door flies open. She's holding a baby, and a toddler is clamped to each leg. Before I manage to open my mouth, however, her phone rings.

"Just a second," she says. "Would you mind taking Vincent?"

To my horror, she hands me the baby. His hands are covered in goo—orange goo. He smiles at me and then turns bright red. A horrible smell wafts up as I feel his diaper get warm. And then I hear what I think is the sound of Charlie's door getting whacked. This is a nightmare.

Harassed Mother is still on the phone. "Yes . . . ," she says. "No! You are *kidding*!"

I make a move to deposit Smelly Vincent on the porch, but he screams and grabs on to my shirt. His mother sounds as if she's going to be awhile yet.

"Maybe," I think to myself, "maybe I can get to Charlie's and back before she notices." I run, taking Smelly Vincent with me.

"Is Charlie home?" His mother is not happy. She looks as if she's just woken up. Then I remember he told me he was going to play baseball.

Before I can apologize for waking her up, I hear loud knocking. It must be Gnome Lady's house. Charlie's mother, though, is still looking at me suspiciously.

"Is that Vincent?" she asks.

"I'm um, um, babysitting. 'Bye for now."

Gnome Lady opens her door when I'm only halfway across the street. I can't run any faster because I don't want to drop the baby.

"Did you knock?" she asks when I finally reach her.

"No!" I yell.

She glances around the cul-de-sac. There's no one else around.

"Yes!" I yell louder. "Because I want to ask your advice."

As you probably know, grown-ups love when children ask for their advice. They get all puffed up and serious. But as I'm furiously thinking of gnome-related questions, such as how to start a collection, or what makes the perfect gnome—a wheelbarrow, a hoe, or a humorous hat—Gnome Lady wrinkles her nose.

"What is that smell?" she asks. "I think that baby needs a diaper change."

Thump, thump, thump. Hedge Man's door again. Elizabeth is really going for it this time.

"Thanks so much for that," I say. "Well, I'd better go and get that done right away. Nice to meet you."

I'm only halfway to Hedge Man's when Charlie's mom answers the knock on her door. It's no use. I stop dead in my tracks. I'm not going to make it.

"Elizabeth!" I shout. "I said I was sorry! Please stop." But does she? Since Harassed Mother's door is wide open, I hear her bell ring twice for good measure. Gnome Lady swings her door open, and then I hear our front door getting a pounding.

So there I am, me and the baby, standing stockstill in the middle of the cul-de-sac. Only Smelly Vincent is laughing.

"What exactly is going on here, young man?" asks Hedge Man.

"I just came off the night shift," says Charlie's mom, "and you woke me up. Twice."

Vincent's mother appears. "What are you doing with my baby?"

"Frank?" says my mom. "What's going on?"

Gnome Lady just shakes her head.

I can't tell them that my sister has officially begun her campaign of chaos. So I say the first thing that comes into my head.

"Friends, neighbors, . . . cul-de-sac dwellers . . . thank you for coming to your doors. I'd like to make an announcement. My name is Frank Black, and my family and I have just moved into number 44." I gesture weakly toward my house. "We'd like to invite you to a housewarming party. Tonight!"

Hedge Man clears his throat.

"After my lesson, of course," I say, "with Mr. Hedge."

A voice whispers in my ear. She's been standing there the whole time.

"His name's Smith, you half-wit," she says.

"Mr. Half-wit . . . I mean Mr. Smith."

My life is a total disaster.

And yet, the party is a great success. I've got to hand it to my parents. They're always up for unexpected socializing. All the neighbors come and, as usual, pretend not to be shocked by Elizabeth's appearance, or lack thereof. And because of my quick thinking and creative problem solving, her Bang and Bolt Routine falls flat. On the downside, I've agreed to regular trimming lessons with Hedge Man and occasional babysitting for Harassed Mother. It looks like this plan of mine is going to be a whole lot harder than I first imagined.

Chapter Three

It's my first day at Grovesdale Junior High School. Since I'm the only new kid, I'm standing in front of my class, and they're all staring up at me. The teacher has just spent the last ten minutes explaining the lunch rotation and the location of every bathroom in the building.

"So now you know about us," says my new teacher. "Why don't you tell us a little bit about yourself?"

I often wonder why people ask you that kind of question. Instantly my mind goes blank.

"Well, where shall I start?" I reply. "First steps, first words, number of broken bones?" I smile. Not a single person smiles back. Somebody coughs. I have a feeling this is not going too well.

"Just tell us about your family," the teacher says. "Brothers? Sisters?"

This is the one new-school moment I always hate the most. I just wish for once I didn't have to launch into my big explanation.

"A sister," I say. "I have a sister."

The homeroom teacher, Mr. Wright (who, judging by the sweat suit and whistle, also teaches gym) waits for more.

"A sister?" he repeats.

"Yes, a sister . . ."

"Older? Younger?"

Clearly he's not going to let the subject go. I take a deep breath and begin.

"Let's put it this way," I start. "Some people are—"

From the hallway I hear the distant but regular sound of locker doors slamming. I try to ignore it and continue.

"Some people are born—"

The banging is getting closer. Kids start shifting in their seats and turning around.

"It's a rare, untreatable condition," I say a little louder. "Called *Formus*—"

The door handle suddenly turns and the door

flies open. A tuna sandwich wrapped loosely in tin-foil flies through the air and hits me on the shoulder.

"You took the wrong sandwich, stupid!" my sister yells. "Now give me the cheese."

I pull out my lunch box and hold the sandwich in midair. It bobs toward the door.

"Thank you," she says before slamming the door behind her.

There's a shocked silence followed by an explosion of laughter. I realize that tuna now covers Mr. Wright's sweat-suit bottoms. He even has a shred of lettuce in his mustache.

"*Formus Disappearus*," I say in a whisper.

"Was *that* your sister?" asks Mr. Wright.

"Her name's Elizabeth," I reply. "She's . . . well, as you can see, or not see, she's . . ."

I would have been fine if she hadn't just turned up and hurled a sandwich at me. I've given this speech a million times before, but she put me off my stride. All I can think about is how long it will be before Mr. Wright notices the lettuce. He's going to hate me. And there's nothing worse than a gym teacher who hates you.

"Is she invisible?" chimes a kid from the back.

"Cool," say several people at the same time.

And then, just like that, the bell rings. Saved.

We all file off to Spanish. Even though it's my first day, so far I like this school. It's a big, modern building, all bricks and glass with an organic vegetable patch behind a baseball diamond. And there's a Rollerblading team. I'm wearing my Darth Vader T-shirt and my green high-tops. I'm looking pretty good, I think. Tons of people want to sit next to me. At first I think it must be my own personal magnetism, but it soon dawns on me that all they want to know about is Elizabeth. They spend all of recess and most of lunch bugging me. Finally, I give them the low-down: there are no rules to my sister's condition. Clothes usually become invisible when she puts them on but not always. Sometimes the objects she touches float in space, and sometimes you can't see them at all. But just when you think you see a pattern, it changes. Even Elizabeth never knows which way it will go.

That's enough explanation for some kids, but others simply will not let it go, asking more and more questions that I obviously can't answer. And so I'm forced to get a little creative just to shut them up.

"And there I was, standing in the burning building, holding the kitten. And I knew my sister was in there somewhere, probably injured, and it was up to me to find her."

Okay, I admit it, occasionally I go too far. But they are hanging on every word.

"Well, did you find her?" one boy asks.

"It cost me everything I had, but I did it." I shrug nonchalantly.

"You are such a liar," comes a voice out of nowhere.

"Elizabeth," I say. "Hey there ... we were just talking about you."

"You couldn't find me if I were standing right next to you," she says. "Which, incidentally, I am."

"Well I ... I ... ," I start. "You owe me a sandwich!"

"Have you told your new friends any true stories, like the time you chained yourself to the banister and had to be rescued by the firemen?"

"That was your fault."

"Yeah right," she says. "See you later."

The crowd around me suddenly disperses. Everyone has a question for her, but no one knows which way she went. Several kids just start talking to the air.

"What's it like to be invisible?"

"Are you wearing any clothes?"

"Have you ever robbed a bank?"

"Can you fly, too?"

"She's gone, guys," I say again. But nobody's listening anymore.

I turn and slink off to the playground. I should have kept my mouth shut. I should have changed the subject.

"Hey, Frank." It's Charlie. "You want to play baseball? We're one man short."

As you know, I hate baseball and everything about it, but I need to do something to take my mind off the humiliation. Thankfully I'm put out in left field, which is great because I don't actually have to do anything, just stand around and do the occasional monkey lope. And then, freakishly, I make two great catches. By the time the bell rings, I'm a hero and no one's talking about Elizabeth anymore.

After school, Elizabeth finds me and we walk home together, just as we'd promised Mom. Of course, my sister is her usual uncommunicative self.

"So," I ask Elizabeth, breaking the silence, "how was your day?"

She doesn't answer.

"I had an awesome time. My new friend Charlie

is in my English class. And my math teacher played classical guitar for us. . . . So, did you make any friends?"

Still nothing.

"Are you even there? If you're not, I'm telling. You know what Mom said."

"I'm here," she replies softly.

We're not even halfway home. And so I try another tack.

"Charlie said the school had an invisible history teacher years and years ago. He fell in love with an invisible tour guide from a museum during a field trip. Neither of them was ever heard from again."

"You have no idea, do you?"

"I've done my fair share of new schools too, you know. It's a nightmare."

"They keep asking me if I'm wearing any clothes," she says. "Like, duh? Do they think I want to freeze to death? Do they think I'm some sort of nudist?"

"Maybe you just have to explain."

"Why? It's just *so* obvious."

"Not really," I say. "Not to everyone—"

"And the teachers are all idiots," Elizabeth interrupts. "One even introduced me as a new face. Everyone laughed. I'm not going to that school."

This conversation is heading in the wrong direction. I try to pull her back.

"The first few days at a new school are always the hardest. Everyone knows that. So . . . any cute boys?"

No reply.

"I don't know," I continue. "I think this might be a good school. The principal seems all right. He came into our room this morning asking students for suggestions. Plus, they have a debate team . . . you like arguing, Elizabeth. Are you listening or am I talking to myself?"

An old man walks past us and looks at me as if I'm insane.

"I'll say," he mutters.

"Excuse me, I was talking to my sister," I point out.

He shakes his head and mumbles something under his breath. I let it go.

"Elizabeth, you still with me?"

"Where else would I be," she says, "China?"

"Please, just stick it out till the end of the semester."

"Keep your hair on," she says, giving me a push. "It's not as if I spent the whole day crying in the bathroom."

We don't talk for the rest of the way home.

Whenever there's a pile of leaves on the sidewalk, they explode violently into the air, each one kicked by an invisible foot. I'm thinking it's pretty likely that she did spend part of her day crying in the bathroom.

It might not seem like a crisis, but let me tell you this: if Elizabeth doesn't like a school, then very soon everyone's going to know about it. In the school before last, food trays floated, clocks were all set to different times, and the chess tournament was ruined when the pieces started dancing. It was pandemonium.

If my plan is going to work, Elizabeth has to like this place as much as I do. All I have to do is make her the most popular girl in school. "*It could happen*," I tell myself over and over, "but what are the chances?"

"Can't you just try?" I beg her. "Just try to like it."

"I'll give it a week," she says as we turn the corner onto Morningvale Circle. "No more, no less."

Chapter Four

In the following days, I figure out where all my classrooms are, I am voted class rep on the student council, and I am even picked for the baseball team. After school, Charlie comes over and we work on the tree house. Though the fate of the tree still has to be decided, we don't let that stop us. The floor is down and we're working on the walls. It's not exactly rainproof, but when it's finished it will have two windows, a door, and a tree stump for a table. Elizabeth shuts herself in her room every night and listens to her crummy boy bands. Of course, Mom and Dad are too busy working to notice. I try to persuade her to sign up for something, anything. Basketball, I suggest. Unfair advantage, she replies. Chess club? Boring. Badminton? Nerd sport.

"Well, how about drama?" I suggest. "I hear they're casting for *My Fair Lady*."

She doesn't even bother to respond to that one.

"Maybe you could do something backstage . . . or special effects?" I mutter. But, of course, it's the Wrong Thing to Say.

"You just don't understand," she says. Her hairbrush slams down on the table so hard I jump. "Nobody notices me, sees me, talks to me. I'm invisible, don't you *get it*? Can you imagine living like this?"

I try to imagine what it must be like. Really, I try. But I can't imagine looking into the bathroom mirror every day and seeing only a corner of shower curtain and a square of wall.

"Now can you get out of my room?" she says. "Or do you have any more stupid suggestions? By the way, the week's almost up."

And then she slams the door behind me so hard that the paint nearly falls off.

. . .

That night, I can't sleep. Every time I close my eyes, I see moving vans and moving boxes and mountains of mail that's never for us. Suddenly I know what I have to do. I have to achieve the impossible. I have to make my invisible sister visible. "Wait a minute," I tell myself. "That's impossible."

"You look tired, Frank," Mom says at breakfast. "You sleep okay?"

I nod and eat my toast. She wouldn't understand. Believe me. I've already tried.

"He always looks like that," says my sister. "Didn't you know you gave birth to one of the living dead?"

"You're so funny," I reply. "But for some reason nobody's laughing . . ."

"Stop it, both of you," says Mom. "I have good news. I've been hired to cater the postconcert party for none other than, wait for it, wait for it . . . Boys-R-Us! And I got you both free tickets. But since I'm working and Dad's working, I can't leave either of you at home by yourselves. If one goes, you both go. Okay?"

"Are you kidding?" shrieks Elizabeth. "They are my all-time favorite band! We're going."

The toast crumbs cascade from my open mouth like styrofoam rocks in a cheap sci-fi movie. This has got to be the worst day of my life so far.

"Frank?" says Mom. "Aren't you a little bit happy?"

"Mom . . . you know I wouldn't be seen dead at a Boys-R-Us concert!"

Even though I'm wearing dark glasses, a baseball cap, and my dad's long black coat, I've still been spotted by some of the girls in my class. So here I am, the only boy surrounded by thousands of screaming girls, with the invisible one screaming the loudest.

Live, this band is even worse than on their recordings. The sound they make is more painful than going to the dentist. The lead singer is a joke. His jeans are the baggiest, his teeth are the whitest, his hair is the blondest. His name, if you can believe it, is Brucy Bruce.

"He's looking at me, he's looking at me!" screams a girl in front.

"No, he's looking at me!" shouts Elizabeth.

The girl turns and sees no one there but me.

"Loser," she says. "Hey, aren't you the new kid in math?"

I shrug and look away. What's the point of denying it? My reputation is ruined anyway.

After they've finally finished the third encore, I turn to Elizabeth, or where Elizabeth is supposed to be—beside me in Row D, Seat 24.

"All right, let's get out of here," I say.

Silence.

"Don't tell me you were dozing too?"

Still no answer. I pat the seat. It's empty. Great, she dumped me at the first opportunity.

The party backstage is in full swing. The members of Boys-R-Us are gorging themselves on Mom's white-chocolate raspberries, slapping one another on the back and uttering meaningless words like "rockin'" and "rad." They've probably never finished a book among them. They don't even play their own instruments, for crying out loud. My sister has the worst taste in music ever.

"Elizabeth," I say out loud, just in case she's listening. "You have the worst taste in music ever."

Right on cue, a CD is thrust into my hand.

"Get him to sign this for me," she says, her fingers digging into my arm. "I bought it especially."

"Get who to sign it for you? All these guys look the same. Does it matter which one?"

"Are you talking to me?" asks a girl wearing too much lip gloss who is standing beside me with a CD in her hand.

"The singer, you dolt," says Elizabeth. "I don't care about the others. Well, not *much*. He's right over there."

Lip Gloss Girl looks alarmed and slinks off.

Mom comes by and—cue more embarrassment—kisses me on the cheek. I try to hand the CD to her.

"Please, Mom?" I ask. "Could you get it signed by the singer?"

"I'm too busy, honey," she says. "But you know what, he's actually really sweet."

And then she disappears into the crowd with a tray of drinks.

"Frank?" says Elizabeth.

"No way," I say. "He's 'really sweet.' Do it yourself."

"It's Brucy Bruce! Please, Frank, I'm begging you."

"Watch my lips. N-O. I've suffered enough for one day. Unless you come up with another offer . . ."

"Okay, I'll give school another week."

"Two and I'll do it."

I admit it: I always like to do a good deed, especially if there's a payoff. And so there I am, hovering with the new Boys-R-Us CD, aptly named *Heaven Help Me*, in my hand, when Brucy Bruce spots me.

"Hey, little dude! It's so great to see a little dude!"

Boy, this guy is smart.

"How'd the show register on the dude-o-meter?"

I hem, I haw . . . well, he did ask.

"Truthfully?"

His smile is blinding me.

"Yeah, little dude!"

He's waiting. Here goes.

"Honestly, I thought the show was a real—"

Without a hint of warning, Elizabeth gives me a mighty push from behind, propelling me straight into the open arms of Brucy Bruce.

"Whoa, dude, you really *are* a big fan."

Before I can get away, he gives me a man-hug, whacking me so hard my sunglasses fly off. To make matters worse, over his shoulder I spot four girls from my class. They're all staring at me with their mouths wide open.

This is the end of my life as I know it. I will never live this down.

"I'd love to sign this for you," he says, taking the CD from me. "Someone get this little dude a T-shirt."

The party finishes early. I'd say it's just as well because this band needs all the beauty sleep it can get. Outside, at the stage door, Elizabeth accosts me.

"Give me that CD," she says.

"Not quite what we agreed," I point out. "We had a deal. The CD is yours, but not until the two weeks are up."

"Yeah right," she says. "Give it to me. I spent $14.99 on that."

She tries to grab it from me, but I'm not letting her have it. I duck, I swerve, I turn, each time miraculously escaping her clutches. And yes, I realize that I must look like a lunatic doing a crazy dodge-dance by myself, but I'm not giving in that easily. Just as she and I twist for the last time, I see the girls from school staring at me from the bus stop across the road. And in that split second, Elizabeth has me from behind and I can smell her shampoo and chewing gum, I can feel the zipper from her invisible boot digging into my shin and the pinching of her bangles on my arm. But she has overestimated my balance; she has used too much force, and rather than hold me still, she propels us forward until we're both falling headlong toward the sidewalk. In slow motion, the CD slips from my hand.

"Nooooo!" we both yell like we're in some action movie and not in a small suburban town outside an empty theater. The CD flies through the air and lands in the middle of the road. Of course, an oncoming bus smashes it into a million pieces.

"So does this mean the deal is off?" I say.

The next day, the principal calls me out of home ec. He wants to "have a word." I don't mind. I need a break from the constant teasing. Those girls made sure the whole school knows about my "special relationship" with Brucy Bruce and my "wacky" solo dancing. Even though I'm wearing my Death Metal T-shirt, it doesn't seem to help.

"Have a seat, Frank," says Mr. Polwarth. He seems harmless enough. I wonder what he wants to talk about. Actually, I have an idea.

"I'd like to speak to you about Elizabeth," he says. "I'm sending a letter to your parents, but I thought maybe we could have a little chat as well."

He talks for a while, but I'm not listening. What has she done now? I have to intercept that letter. If Mom and Dad get wind of any trouble, who knows where it could lead.

"Frank? Have you been listening to a word I've been saying?"

"Don't tell me," I reply. "Is it the Lunch Lady Bait and Switch Trick?"

He gives me a puzzled look.

"The Dancing Chalk?"

He still looks blank.

"Oh, please tell me it's not the Lock and Leave Toilet Trick."

By the look on his face, I think I should probably shut up now.

"You mean she's not in trouble?"

"Not as far I know . . ."

"Has she been skipping school?"

"No, Frank, her attendance is excellent and her grades are generally good. She's a bright and polite student."

"No, no, you have her mixed up with someone else." I stand up. "My sister is Elizabeth Black, the invisible one."

"Frank! Relax. Sit down." He gestures toward the chair. "We want every student in our school to feel like a part of the wider community. Our sense is that Elizabeth is not fitting in as well as she could be. I've tried talking to her, tried getting her to join some clubs, but frankly, Frank"—he pauses and laughs at his own joke. If only he knew how many times I've heard that one—"I'm not getting anywhere. Do you have any ideas?"

I think about this.

"Just because she's invisible," I say, "doesn't mean that she has to be, well, invisible."

The equipment arrives the very next day. I get time off from class to help Mr. Polwarth set it all up. Although it's officially for the media club, he and I have our own agenda. I even manage to convince him that a letter home won't be necessary.

"I'm not interested," says Elizabeth.

"Well, you will be when I tell you what I set up."

Elizabeth is interested. She's so interested that she even threatens to kiss me. Also, she agrees to my demands. Giving the school a little longer has been forgotten—there's no question of her wanting to leave right now. Instead she agrees to be my slave for a day and that the big tree in the yard stays.

It's a week later, and my sister has kept her word. Yesterday I sent her to the store for two megasized jawbreakers, a bag of dog biscuits for Bob, and the latest copy of my favorite comic. She brought me breakfast in bed this morning, but I was too nervous to eat it. I'm not the only one. Mom has been reading the classified ads since I came home from school, and

Dad has been in the garage endlessly tinkering with his fishing rods. At last, at four o'clock exactly, we all sit down on the couch and Mom turns on the radio.

"Good afternoon, this is Elizabeth Black broadcasting loud and clear from KGJH, Grovesdale Junior High School's new state-of-the-art radio station. My first guest is none other than Brucy Bruce, patched in live from New York City . . ."

We shouldn't have worried. Elizabeth is in her element. The interview goes off without a hitch. By the end, even *I* think there's more to Boys-R-Us than meets the eye. And then he has to go and spoil it.

"Before I sign off," says her special guest, "I have a shout-out going to the little dude, Frank Black. Brucy Bruce loves you too, man."

So I've succeeded in making Elizabeth visible, at least for a little while. But I'll tell you one thing— right now, I wish I were the invisible one instead.

Chapter Five

It's finally Halloween. For weeks, all Charlie has been talking about is his zombie costume. He's already gone through several tubes of fake blood, staged a car accident, and had a couple of amputations. And now he's so excited he can hardly wait until nightfall.

"You want to come over and help me put the finishing touches on my costume?"

"I can't," I tell him. "I'm babysitting for Smelly Vincent's mom. Well, not exactly babysitting. She's going to be in the attic office working, but she needs me to keep an eye on the kids. She promised that she won't be more than a couple of hours."

Yes, ever since my sister's atrocious Bang and Bolt Routine a week after we moved in, I've had to put on my best-neighbor-ever face. Babysitting? I love it! Hedges? My passion! Gnomes? Uh . . . so . . . so . . . so cute, I lie. I'm beginning to wonder just how much longer I can keep it up.

"But your costume," says Charlie. "You haven't finished it."

I've been working on my Impaled Airplane-Pilot Crash Victim costume for about a month. I have all the parts: the uniform complete with cap, the control stick (which will be protruding from my stomach), and an extra-large package of latex stick-on wounds, all courtesy of eBay.

Charlie said it will be the grossest thing ever and he should know; he's the King of Gross.

As Charlie pointed out, however, it still needs a lot of work. I haven't decided exactly how to get the control stick to look like it's going right through me.

"You're going to be able to finish in time, aren't you?" asks Charlie. "I don't want to have to go by myself."

"Of course," I reply. "She gave me her word."

. . .

Smelly Vincent's house has a jack-o'-lantern pumpkin on the porch. When I walk in, I'm bombarded by a hail of tiny plastic spiders.

"Ooooooh!!" the children all shriek, trying to be scary. It's not even dark yet and they are already hyper.

"Frank," says Smelly Vincent's mom, "I'm so grateful to you for this. I know it is short notice, but I have to finish some paperwork. Can you possibly give the kids a hand putting on their costumes? They're so looking forward to going trick-or-treating."

I have a few questions for her, like how many snacks are too many snacks and should the TV really be that loud, but she sneaks up the stairs when the kids aren't looking. And then they all start crying because they seriously believe she's gone forever and they are being left for eternity with the loser boy from next door.

"Don't worry," I yell in an effort to calm them down. "Didn't she tell you that I turn into a ghost at midnight? . . . OOOoooh . . ."

But that just makes them bawl even louder. I start over.

"This must be yours," I say to Laura, holding up a very pink, very frilly princess costume in an attempt to distract her.

"I changed my mind. I'm too old to be a princess," she says, her sobs turning into sniffs.

"Why? How old are you?" I ask.

"Six and three quarters. And I want to be a cowboy."

"Where's the cowboy costume?"

"We don't have one, so you'll have to make it."

"Okay . . . we'll come back to you later."

Joey and Lucy are twins. They're three. I recognize their costumes from a buy one, get one free deal at the local supermarket: one devil, one angel. Sounds simple? Think again.

"Which one of you is the devil?"

"I am," says Joey.

"No, I am," says Lucy.

"I had it first," screams Joey, grabbing the pitchfork.

"No, I did," screams Lucy, throwing the angel wings at Joey.

And then they both start crying again at full volume. This is a nightmare. I close my eyes and wonder how long I can stand it. I've only been here for ten minutes and I'm temped to quit. *Snap* goes the pitchfork as it's broken in two. *Rip* go the angel wings as they're yanked from their elastic.

"Waaahhh!" go the twins.

Pete, who's about five, has been pulling on my shirt and repeating "Excuse me, excuse me, excuse me," for the last few minutes. Finally, he kicks me in the shin.

"Ow!" I cry out. "What was that for?"

"Excuse me!" screams Pete.

"What is it?" I scream back.

"I can't find my donkey costume."

"Where's the last place you saw it?"

"In the dress-up box."

"Okay," I say as calmly as I can. "Let's go and look for it."

I pull everything out of the box. It's not there. The closest things I can find are a tiger suit and the bottom half of a zebra.

"Here you go," I say cheerfully.

"That's not a donkey, it's a tiger."

"Is it? Well, it's a very donkeyish kind of tiger."

"It's a tiger, stupid."

"Laura! Where's the donkey outfit?"

"We don't have one," she says. "You'll have to make it. But only after you make my cowboy costume. And I'd like some juice now. In my favorite cup. I'll take it here." And then she flops down on the couch, turns on the TV with the remote, and starts to watch the shopping channel.

I try not to lose my temper, but it's getting harder by the second. And so I dig down for my big grown-up voice.

"Just a minute, young lady."

"And it has to be very cold, otherwise I won't drink it."

I'm speechless. Who does she think I am? I'm not even getting paid for this. The twins are still fighting. Pete is sulking in the corner, methodically pulling out clumps of fur from the tiger suit, and Smelly Vincent is . . . where *is* Smelly Vincent?

I rush from room to room. After frantically searching the entire house, I finally find him in the laundry room. He's about to plunge a large screwdriver into a wall socket.

"Stop!" I scream.

"Stop!" Vincent screams right back at me.

I wrench the screwdriver from his tiny fingers. The handle's all covered in snot.

Having saved Vincent's life, I take a long, deep breath. "I can do this," I tell myself. "It's only baby-sitting, not brain surgery." I plunk the baby down in the playpen for safekeeping, get Laura's juice, separate the twins, and pull out the craft box. "If I can make Impaled Airplane-Pilot Crash Victim," I tell myself, "I can make anything."

After what feels like a week, I have created one psycho cowboy, one demented donkey, and a couple of robots. (It's amazing what you can do with tinfoil, a glue stick, and some cardboard boxes.) By the time I get to Smelly Vincent's, I'm on a roll. Dressed in a sheet with a string of plastic ivy on his head, he is a perfect Roman baby.

"You guys look *fantastic*," I enthuse. Laura doesn't look convinced.

"I'm not so sure about the hat." She tries to adjust the swimming cap with its cardboard brim. "And these cowboy boots hurt." I customized her rubber boots by pinching a couple of clothespins on the backs for spurs. They look great, but they must be killing her.

"I think I want to be a princess after all."

The doorbell rings. It's Charlie in full zombie getup.

"You still here?"

"No," I reply. "I'm an illusion created from your own distorted imagination."

"Very funny. We gotta go."

"I'm heading out now!" I shout up the stairs to the attic. I have been here two hours after all.

"Oh, Frank," shouts Harassed Mother, "I'm not quite finished up here. Are you going trick-or-treating?"

You can hear us coming from the end of the street. Charlie (in full character) groaning in agony, Laura clacking her clothespin spurs, the twins in their crunchy tinfoil outfits, and Smelly Vincent gurgling like a drain.

"Give me five minutes, Charlie," I say when we reach my house. "I'll just run in and put on my costume."

I try to hand him the baby.

"No way—I don't want baby drool to ruin my perfectly splattered blood."

One of the twins bursts into tears.

"My tinfoil is tearing."

"Stop pulling on my tail!"

"You're standing on my toe!"

Just then our front door opens. There's no one there.

"You're not busy, are you?" I yell over the din.

Elizabeth drives a hard bargain: half my trick-or-treat loot for an hour's work. But I'm desperate.

"It's not likely you are going to get much, looking like that," she says. "I've seen senior citizens in the

50

grocery store who look scarier than you. And what's the baby supposed to be, anyway?"

But there's no time to argue or explain. I thrust Smelly Vincent into her arms, leave Elizabeth to introduce herself, and rush upstairs to get changed.

It could have been the best costume ever. It could have been really, really gross. But you try being Impaled Airplane-Pilot Crash Victim when there's a crowd of small children yelling at you to hurry up.

"I know what you are," Laura says when I come downstairs. For a split second, I actually believe it's better than I hoped.

"This is what you get when you don't change your mind at the last minute," I tell her. "A costume like this takes weeks of preparation and skill. You scared?"

"Why would I be scared of a boy covered in duct tape, holding an old steering wheel?"

"Maybe you should have used more of the wounds and less of the tape," says Charlie with a sigh. "Look at us. This is going to be the worst Halloween ever."

We start three streets away. By the time we reach the end of the block, our bags are almost a quarter full. Charlie's pessimism was clearly unfounded. We may be stuck with four little kids, but we're still getting results. I almost forget about Elizabeth until she whispers in my ear.

"Don't take so many Snickers bars. You know I hate them."

At the next house, the door opens before we get a chance to ring the bell. Out come a Dracula, two Grim Reapers, and the Four Horsemen of the Apocalypse. Their garbage bags are bulging, and it's not even six thirty.

"Your costumes stink," they say as they brush past.

The old couple inside look traumatized. Their floor is littered with empty candy wrappers.

"I'm afraid we're all out of treats," says the old lady. "I love your mailman costume."

Charlie laughs so hard I think he'll wet his pants.

Then she smiles at him. "And you, young lady, what are you supposed to be?"

From that moment on, every house we try has already been cleaned out of candy. The ghouls always seem to have been there first. Laura can't hold back the tears.

"Let's just go home," says Charlie. "Under the circumstances, we've done pretty well."

I hoist Smelly Vincent over my shoulder, and

he promptly falls asleep. He's much heavier than he looks, and he starts to drool down my neck. The twins are so tired that they've stopped fighting and have started sucking their thumbs.

Laura is still sniffling. "I want more candy. I *need* more candy."

It's totally dark now, and the people in some of the houses have turned out their lights, pretending they're not in. But just as we reach the edge of our cul-de-sac, seven black shapes pounce from behind Hedge Man's garage. We're surrounded.

"Hand over your bags, and no one gets hurt."

It's one of the Grim Reapers we passed earlier. The tallest of the Four Horsemen of the Apocalypse swaggers over to Laura and snatches her bag out of her hand. She's so stunned, she's speechless.

"Come on, guys, she's just a little kid," I say.

The Dracula turns to me. "What's with the baby, loser? Is that part of your *costume*?"

He smells of deodorant and sour-cream-and-onion potato chips. Everyone bursts into tears at once, including Charlie. As the tallest Horseman is grabbing the rest of the bags, one by one, Smelly Vincent is gently lifted from my shoulder.

"Elizabeth?" I whisper.

"Shhhhh."

In front of my eyes, the baby floats forward, his drool glistening in the moonlight and his Roman toga billowing in the wind. He wakes up and starts to scream. No wonder. It must be pretty freaky to be lifted up by an invisible person.

The Halloween ambushers turn even whiter than their makeup; drop all the loot, including their own; and, to everyone's surprise, run away.

"Who's scared now?" yells Charlie. "Happy Halloween!"

"Think that will be enough candy for you, Laura?" asks Elizabeth.

By the time Harassed Mother finishes her paperwork, all the bags have been emptied, categorized, and counted: 642 assorted chocolate bars, 65 packets of M&M's, and 175 bags of jelly beans.

"I feel sick," says Laura.

"Me too," says Charlie.

Charlie and I have worked out a theory. The more candy you have, the less you want to eat it.

"You can have it all," says Elizabeth as she heads out the front door. "But you still owe me big-time."

Even though Charlie and I only have a short walk

home, there's something creepy in the air. Suddenly, out of the darkness, a bodiless Grim Reaper mask flies toward us. We both scream.

"Elizabeth!" I howl.

"Gotcha, wimps."

I walk Charlie to his front door. It seems only polite, under the circumstances.

"Sorry, Charlie. Sorry about tonight."

"What do you mean? This has been the best Halloween ever!"

He whacks me on the shoulder, and we're suddenly both splattered in fake blood.

"What was that?" I ask.

"My exploding vein-popping mechanism. I totally forgot to use it. Do you like it? How about we use it next year? We can be the Exploding-Blood Brothers."

"It's awesome," I say.

"Well?" he asks expectantly.

I suddenly feel a little sad. I would like to say sure, why not. But I don't want to promise Charlie anything. If my plan doesn't work out and my family behaves the way they usually do, the chances of me still being here next Halloween are virtually zip.

"Maybe," I tell him. "Maybe . . ."

Chapter Six

As I said, I used to wish that my dad worked in an office all week. And that my mom spent all day at home in an apron baking pies and making her own bread. Yes, I was desperate for the kind of family that organized perfect picnics on perfect summer days: happy, ordinary, and respectable. But then I grew up and realized that my family is like most other families, a combination of totally weird and absolutely unique. Although mine might be tipping the scales in the weird department.

Take Dad. When he isn't fine dining, he's

rehearsing. He plays lead guitar for a retro punk band he formed called the Spits. The band members may change but the racket they make always stays the same. It would be less embarrassing if Dad would lose the ripped T-shirt and crummy plastic jeans. Mom says it's sexy. I say it's in very poor taste. That's the whole point, stupid, says my sister.

To Elizabeth's horror, Dad has signed up the Spits to be in the school talent contest. She's spent the last week begging him to withdraw.

"I may look old to you," he tells her. "But in here"—and he thumps his chest—"I'm seventeen."

That chest, I tell you, has seen a lot of thumping.

A cushion flies through the air. Dad tries to dodge it, but it hits him square in the stomach.

"Right," my sister says. "But you have the reflexes of someone who's eighty-two."

"I don't know why you didn't sign up yourself, honey," Mom tells Elizabeth. "You have such a beautiful singing voice."

"I don't think so," she says.

"Sure you do, honey," Dad agrees. "Why don't you help me load the car? And then you could come and watch the gig. It'll be a hoot."

"I wouldn't be seen dead with you looking like

that," she says. "Dad, I'd never be able to show my face in school again."

"*Ha!*" I blurt.

This comes out of my mouth completely involuntarily. I follow it with a fake cough, but Elizabeth isn't buying it.

The pain is instantaneous: two hands wrap around my arm, followed by sharp twists in opposite directions. Always deadly. Always effective.

Dad grabs a microphone stand and is on the way out to the car. As usual, he sees nothing.

"Aaaah!" I yell.

"Rooms, both of you," says Mom, who has overheard the whole thing. "Now."

"That's not fair," I reply. It's my stock response. It never changes anything.

"Rooms!" shouts Mom.

From my bedroom window, I watch my dad load the car alone. As he's closing the trunk, Mom calls to him.

"Honey," she says. "A quick word?"

Mom's quick words are never quick. I sneak out to the top of the stairs to try and overhear, but they close the door. I think she's worried that Grovesdale Junior High isn't ready for an act of Dad's "caliber." Twenty minutes later, the door flies open again.

"It will all be fine," says Dad. "Don't worry."

"So you guarantee: no stage diving, no guitar smashing, and you'll keep it all PG," says Mom.

"Why don't I be a roadie?" I suggest. "That way I can keep an eye on him from backstage."

"I don't think that will stop him," whispers Mom. "But you have my permission to pull the plug if it gets to be too much."

We meet the rest of the band in the school parking lot. Boy, do they look sad. If my dad is seventeen going on eighty-two, the other guys are fifty going on one hundred. I always hate seeing them in their outfits; they look like shrink-wrapped prunes.

"We're gonna rock their socks right off," says Rod, the bass player. I stifle a snicker. His socks are of a particularly unappealing fluorescent toweling variety.

And then catastrophe strikes. Dad opens the trunk. It's empty. No guitars, no microphones, no nothing. The show is about to start. The Spits are on second. They stare at Dad. Dad shakes his head in disbelief.

"It was all in there," he insists. "I loaded it myself."

They all stare into the trunk as if everything will rematerialize if only they look hard enough.

"What's that?" asks Rod.

A note is attached to the floor with masking tape.

"Sorry. I just couldn't let this happen," reads Rod.

You can imagine what happens next. The other band members start to shout, using words that are absolutely off limits for a school parking lot. You'd have thought they were playing Radio City Music Hall in New York City, not the auditorium of a small suburban junior high school. And then they all storm off, back to their dented little Ford Fiestas.

"Wow," Dad says. "Elizabeth really didn't want me to play this gig. Maybe she's not happy here. Do you think it's the school? Or maybe it's this town?"

He sits on the curb, his head in his hands.

"You're just going to give up?" I ask. "You're going to quit? The whole evening's been planned out. The programs have already been printed."

"But what can I do without my guitar?" he asks.

"Don't you have anything at all?"

He looks in his pockets and pulls out a kazoo.

"I have this," he says, "but there's no way I can sing and play at the same time."

The auditorium is standing room only. As the curtain goes up, I wonder if I've made a horrible mistake. But you know what? Once I start playing, it's actually kind of fun. By the end we are totally rocking, in a kazooish kind of way.

Our rendition of "La Bamba" comes in second place. We were robbed. Oscar White from the eighth grade wins. His "tap dancing" was a total joke, but the judges were swayed by the enormous effort he obviously put into his ridiculously sparkly costume.

"That was a blast," someone from my class calls out as we walk back to the car.

"Thanks," I say. I have a short but convincing vision of becoming the most popular boy in my class.

"Celebratory fast food?" Dad offers.

"Absolutely," I reply.

I climb into the front seat, and Dad gets behind the wheel.

"You looked like a jerk, Frank," comes a voice from the back.

"Elizabeth! So you saw us play?" Dad asks.

"Hey, aren't you mad at her?" I ask.

"But it was fun." He laughs. "And maybe the school wasn't ready for the Spits, anyway."

"See?" Elizabeth agrees. "I did this family a favor."

"I wouldn't go that far," Dad says. "So how about that burger?"

"I hate that kind of food," my sister replies. "Can't we go somewhere else?"

"Not fair," I say. "You don't get to choose."

To stop the bickering, Dad takes us to his favorite Japanese restaurant. He knows we both love sushi.

On the way home, Dad hums our winning tune.

"Come on, Frank," he says. "Once more, for old time's sake."

We both sing at the top of our lungs. Even Elizabeth joins in.

"Mom was right," I tell her, "you do have a good voice. Why don't you enter next year?"

There's a silence, and I can tell everyone's thinking the same thing. This family doesn't really do long-term planning.

Chapter Seven

It's a cloudless fall day, the kind of day when boys like me should be out playing baseball, with their dads cheering them on from the bleachers. But I'm not that kind of boy and my dad's not that kind of dad. Mom's baking white-chocolate muffins, the not-for-you-so-don't-eat-them kind, and singing along to the radio. The tree house is almost finished, but Charlie isn't around to work on it. And so Bob and I are making a skateboard ramp out of cinder blocks and old wood. Then we rake up all the leaves and fly off the ramp into the piles. Totally radical stuff. It is, in other words, a perfect day.

"*What a perfect day*," I start to sing.

"It would be if you weren't around to spoil my view," says Elizabeth. "You're all covered in leaves. How do you know you haven't rolled in any dog poop? You certainly smell as if you did. You too, Bob."

Bob barks twice. Sometimes I wonder what life would be like without my sister. Just me and Mom and Dad. And Bob (who, of course, wouldn't dream of pooping in our leaves). It would be a restful, beautiful life. No drama, no tantrums, no sarcastic comments coming out of thin air. I would be an only child, in the loving arms of my devoted parents.

Bob is staring up at me, and I know what he's thinking: "Dream on, kid."

As if on cue, Dad begins to yell.

"Everybody, family meeting, my office, *now*!"

Dad's "office" is a small space on the landing at the top of the stairs. There's a table and one bookshelf, but most of his stuff is pinned up on the walls or piled up on the floor. We sit on the stairs while he addresses us from his secondhand swivel chair.

"I'd just like to remind you guys that nobody touches anything in my work space."

You'd think by the way he says it that his office is six times the size, has a view of the Empire State

Building, and comes with a secretary. In reality, it's something to trip over on the way to the bathroom.

"I recently lost some very important documents," he says with a serious expression.

"Don't look in my direction, Dad," says Elizabeth. "Mom found that check in your coat pocket."

Dad clears his throat. "Nevertheless, all I'm saying is that I have a career to think about. This may look like junk to you, but it's all part of my ongoing research."

A laminated menu floats in midair.

"I know, I know, I review restaurants." Dad sighs and rubs his eyes. "But this is only a temporary measure. Today, the relative merits of shrimp cocktail. Tomorrow, the unraveling of a political scandal. Anyway, just don't touch my stuff. Okay?"

When Dad was a kid, he dreamed of becoming a first-rate investigative reporter—the Sherlock Holmes of the newspaper world. He's still waiting for his big break. It's not that he doesn't try. Dad's constantly digging around, following leads, and asking difficult questions, and he is always, always just on the brink of front-page news. And yet it never seems to happen. Impossible deadlines, unreliable sources, changes in newspaper editors . . . but mostly, I have to say, it's the constant moving that gets in the way. In other words, Elizabeth.

"Is this meeting over?" asks Elizabeth.

"Yes, this meeting is now adjourned. I have some work to do. Then it's off to Chow Man Fat for dinner. It's a midnight deadline, kids, so I'd appreciate it if you'd stay out of my hair."

"Didn't that place just close down?" Elizabeth asks as she heads down the stairs.

"If it had closed down," he says, "would I be reviewing it? Duh!"

I shudder. I hate it when Dad uses the same expressions I do. It just doesn't sound cool. It would be like me telling him to stop being "inappropriate."

Bob and I are lying on my bed reading the latest *Dog World* (he likes the pictures) when I see a slight flicker of color on the wall. It must be the reflection of the sunlight streaming through the trees outside. Then I notice one of my *Star Wars* figures is moving. I pretend to read, but over the top of my comic I watch the figures on my shelf change places. Elizabeth is just trying to start something. She knows how much time I spent bidding for those guys on eBay.

"Elizabeth, is your life so empty that you can

think of nothing better to do than shift figures around on a shelf?"

"I found this on the floor in the hall," she says. "And I was just putting it back for you. Lighten up!"

"Yeah, right."

Before she has time to deny it, Mom shouts up the stairs. "Elizabeth, will you stop messing with the window? It took me all morning to write these invitations and now they've blown all over the floor."

Suddenly Dad's voice booms down the hallway. "Elizabeth, where's my tape? Honestly, this is getting ridiculous."

I look over and see the tape from Dad's desk on my worktable, where I left it. I'm thinking about keeping my mouth shut.

"Why is everything always my fault?" Elizabeth yells. "If something goes wrong or gets lost or gets broken in this house, everybody always assumes it's me!"

"That's so not true. Just think about it for a minute!" I yell back. "I'm the one who gets blamed for everything around here. You always make sure of that. Admit it, Elizabeth."

My door slams, and she thunders down the hall and out the front door.

As you've probably guessed by now, my sister is a number one storm-outer, a first-class slammer, an excellent sulker. I sometimes wonder what she does when she leaves. Does she sit on park benches next to people whose problems make hers look trivial? Or does she go to expensive shops and leave her fingerprints on all the things kids are not supposed to touch? Or does she just walk around looking in people's windows? She never says what she's been doing but whatever it is, it seems to work. She usually returns thirty minutes later, walking in as if nothing had happened.

It's been two hours this time and there's still no sign of her.

Dad's already in his reviewing outfit. He tries to go incognito, but he still stands out. Apart from the fact that no one wears corduroy jackets and paisley cravats anymore, he seems to forget that his photo appears every week at the top of his column, only slightly disguised by a fedora.

Mom's dinner is ruined, and she's gone through the three stages of motherly anxiety in no particular order: worry, more worry, and frantic cleaning. Normally I take advantage of Elizabeth's absences. I relax, I play my favorite music without fear of retaliation, or Bob and I do some boy-dog bonding without her predictable teasing. But this time even I'm beginning to get a little nervous.

"She knew I was making goat cheese soufflé; she even said she couldn't wait to try it. And now look at it."

We all look at Mom's dish. Instead of light and airy, it looks flat and soggy, like a cake that's been left out in the rain.

"I'm sure it will be delicious, honey. It's just a little . . . deflated," says Dad.

The window in the kitchen flies open, and for a moment we think it's her.

"Honey?" says Mom.

No answer.

"Look, these hinges are broken," says Dad. "They're totally rusted. Elizabeth didn't have anything to do with your invitations blowing all over the place."

"I feel just terrible," says Mom. "I was too quick to blame her."

"But she took the tape," says Dad. "I know she took the tape."

I feel compelled to come clean.

"Dad, I took your tape," I say. "I'm sorry."

He gives me a look. I feel about six inches tall.

"Something could have happened to her," Mom says, sitting down at the table and clutching a dish towel. "She could be lying in some gutter, and no one would ever know she was there."

"Until a car drives over her," I point out.

"Frank!" shout Mom and Dad in unison.

Suddenly the house feels really empty with just the three of us in it.

"Okay," says Mom. "We have to go out and look for her."

"What about Dad's restaurant review?"

"I'll deal with that later," he says.

"I'm going to ask the neighbors to give us a hand," says Mom.

"Do we have to?" I ask. Mom and Dad glare at me. "I mean, do you think it's really necessary to involve the whole neighborhood?"

"Don't be silly, Frank, this is an emergency," says Mom.

We go our separate ways. Charlie and I do the immediate vicinity, and Mom and Harassed Mother take the kids downtown. Dad and Mr. Hedge hit the football field where the teenagers like to hang out, and Gnome Lady stays home to hold down the fort and answer the phone.

"Let's try the tree house," says Charlie.

"She would never go up there," I answer. "She hates that tree."

Charlie and I run around the neighborhood calling Elizabeth's name, trailing our hands along benches, kicking at bushes, and groping at corners. I know we look like weirdos, but tonight I don't care. What if she has really run away, or what if she's hurt? What if she's lying right in front of me and I don't even know it?

I start to tell Charlie what a great sister she can be sometimes: about the day she held me up and stopped me from falling over when we went ice-skating, and how nobody knew. Or the time she tripped a kid who always had it in for me and made him go flying into a puddle. And the way she used to read me stories when I was little and Mom was working late. The more I talk about it, the more I think I might miss her after all.

"Yeah, she seems all right," says Charlie, "for a girl."

"Elizabeth!" I shout. "Where are you?"

Nowhere, it seems. She's totally vanished.

We all meet back at the house an hour later, as planned.

"Nothing?" asks Mom.

"Not a sign," I reply.

"I made hot chocolate," says Gnome Lady. "Anyone want a cup?"

Nobody answers.

"Before we call the police," says Hedge Man, "are we all sure we've looked everywhere?"

"We didn't check the tree house," says Charlie.

"There's no way she's in the tree house," I say.

Everyone files outside and stands underneath the tree. There's a small light inside.

"Well," says Dad. "Are you going to go up and take a look?"

I climb up into the tree house, and there she is. A flashlight floating in midair shines on an open book. An empty bag of potato chips lies on the floor. She's probably been here the whole time. I don't know whether to punch her or hug her.

"What?" she asks, annoyed.

"We've been looking for you for over two hours," I say.

"You have?" she says.

"Elizabeth, are you up there?" Mom shouts from below.

"Yeah, Mom, what's the big deal?"

"She never came up here before," I say weakly. "She despises this tree."

"Since when?" she asks. "I would have thought this would be the first place that any normal person would look."

Everyone stares in her general direction. And then they glare at me.

"False alarm, everybody!" says Dad cheerfully. "Thanks again for your hard work."

The neighbors all say they were happy to help, but as everyone leaves, they don't look too happy to me.

"Oh my goodness, my deadline," whispers Dad as we all head into our house. "I have to turn in this review by midnight."

"But Dad," I remind him, "she made you miss your reservation."

"In life, son," he says, "you have to keep your priorities straight."

"As long as she's safe," says Mom as she brings a mug of steaming hot chocolate to Elizabeth. "That's all that matters."

I think I'm going to vomit.

"But Dad, the review? What about your career?"

"Oh, it's no big deal, I've been there before," says Dad. "I'll just make it up."

I can't believe my ears. My sister has gotten away with it again.

"Miss me, Frank?" my sister asks.

"You hid up there on purpose," I say, "to make all the neighbors hate us."

"They don't hate us, Frank. But right now, I don't think they're too fond of you."

Chapter Eight

It's only November, but Elizabeth has been playing Christmas songs on her school radio show for a week and a half. It's just as bad on Morningvale Circle. Smelly Vincent's front window is plastered with giant paper snowflakes. Hedge Man has started to rig up his festive lights—a high-class technical spectacle, he's been telling everyone—which will illuminate his entire house, yard, and garage. Gnome Lady has already set up her annual Christmas scene. All the main players are there: the three wise men, Mary and Joseph, and the shepherds, all set inside a miniature plastic stable. But despite the biblical costumes, they're all gnomes. With hats. And beards. Even baby Jesus lying in his cradle is just a gnome wrapped up—you can still see the beard. It would be hilarious if it weren't quite so disturbing.

Only Charlie's house and our house haven't succumbed to Christmas madness. Although, according to Charlie, it's just a matter of time before his mother produces the half-price inflatable reindeer that she bought on sale in June.

Every year Dad gives his lecture about the commercialization of the festive season, but the truth is, even if we wanted to join in, we just don't have any of the right stuff. Our Christmas lights haven't worked in years, the ornaments are mostly smashed, and all we have left from last year are the gingerbread cookies Mom baked to decorate the tree.

"Oooh, you're not going to eat that, are you?" Elizabeth shouts at me. "That's not green frosting—it's mold, you moron."

The reason for the premature decorating frenzy is the annual Jingle Bell Jamboree, a competition that celebrates all that is wrong with Christmas. First prize is a cheesy trophy and a gift certificate to the local gardening store. But, according to Charlie, the prize is incidental. It's really about the pride factor. Morningvale Circle has received an "Honorable Mention" every year since the competition began. Hedge Man has been telling anyone who will listen that this year will be different. This year—cue grouchy old man voice—it's ours for the taking.

"He doesn't sound like that," my sister says.

Now that old Doctor Powers from the next street over has been moved to a nursing home, Hedge Man is convinced that victory is within our grasp. Doc Powers's pyrotechnic Santa (with soundtrack) and holographic sleigh were more than legendary. They won his street first prize for four years in a row.

To make sure we win outright, Hedge Man has a plan.

"My young friend, I have one word for you. . . ." He looks at me expectantly.

"Y-y-yes?" I stutter.

"Topiary."

"You mean . . . like . . . hedges?" I ask.

Hedge Man stares into the distance but doesn't reply. You'd think he was Leonardo da Vinci contemplating the *Mona Lisa*, rather than a zealous trimmer of foliage.

"I invite you to assist," he says.

I hesitate. I've had three lessons from Mr. Hedge and every single moment was so boring I thought I was going to die. But since Elizabeth's disappearing act, I've noticed that the neighbors have been a touch distant. Maybe this could be a way to change all that.

"Sure," I reply. "Can I bring a friend?"

And so Charlie and I are instructed to assemble at HQ (Mr. H's garden shed) at 0900 hours on a rainy Saturday morning. We're sitting on overturned flowerpots in front of a giant whiteboard that looks as if it were last used for some business conference. Such is the secrecy of this project (Operation Tinsel—his idea) that Mr. H insists we all have code names. Although Charlie and I came up with loads of really cool ones, Mr. H vetoed them all. While he's called General Xmas, we've been assigned the names Elf One and Elf Two. We're not happy.

"Before we partake of some refreshment"—he gestures toward a table where three graham crackers sit marooned on a plate—"let's take a quick look at our timetable."

He hands Charlie and me bound booklets about half an inch thick. Inside he has mapped out a day-by-day plan that leads up to the eve of the competition, which he then goes into. In great detail. An hour later, our heads are swimming with dates, times, and what seem like a thousand complicated and contradictory tasks.

"You keep mentioning our secret weapon," says Charlie. "What exactly is it?"

"Be patient, Elf Two," says Mr. H. "All will be revealed shortly. Come outside; I want to show you something."

Charlie and I stand in the center of a perfectly manicured backyard.

"What do you think, boys?" he asks proudly.

I scan the place, not sure what I'm looking for. Apart from the hedges, there are a couple of bushes, a birdbath, and several small trees.

"Of what?" asks Elf Two.

General X looks at him as if he's half-witted.

"Run into the shed and get my notepad," he tells Charlie. "Well, Elf One, surely you can appreciate our material in its raw and majestic state."

He motions his hand toward a large and not particularly majestic bush in a pot. I hear a snicker. I wouldn't be surprised if my sister were listening in. I suddenly want to laugh too, and I have to bite my lip to hold it in. Charlie comes back with the notepad.

"The secret weapon, Elf Two, is this."

He opens his book to reveal a detailed drawing.

"That's impossible," I say.

"'Impossible' isn't a word we use in Operation Tinsel. With our grit and determination, my skill, and your youthful enthusiasm, we can make something *awesome*!"

We stare at him blankly.

"I'd say," he goes on, "we all deserve a treat."

We troop back inside the hut. The plate is there, but the graham crackers are gone.

"What?" asks Charlie. "Why are you looking at me? I didn't take them. I don't even like that kind of crummy cookie."

Mr. H shakes his head.

"Elf Two, if I can't trust you with graham crackers, then I can't trust you with our secret. I'm sorry, son. You're off the project."

Charlie has stopped talking to me. But since he got fired, I've been so busy that I haven't had time to work it out. I've been fertilizing, watering, feeding, and even singing to Mr. H's prized bush.

"Hey, bushy babe," I whisper. "Any new shoots today?"

Sometimes I think I'm going crazy. This bush has become my new best friend. But the more the bush grows, the more I see myself as an indispensable and possibly prizewinning member of this neighborhood.

"Elf One!" shouts General X from his porch. "She's looking a little parched today. Try two parts green tea to one part H_2O. And remember, be very careful down there. Her trunk is slender and you don't want to snap her."

"Hello, honey bush," I whisper. "Who's a good little girl?"

"It's a plant," says Elizabeth in my ear. "I worry about you, Frank."

It's the evening before the Jingle Bell Jamboree judges arrive. The street is so brightly lit you can probably see it from the moon: flashing bulbs in every color, spotlighted mangers, and Christmas trees sparkling with twinkling lights in every living room. Everyone is out burnishing their holly with furniture polish and spraying their windows with fake snow. Even my parents caught the festivity virus a week ago and have spent the last five nights making paper chains and candy-cane angels.

"Ho, ho, ho!" cries Mr. H as he hands out formal invitations to the unveiling of our secret weapon. "See you all at six thirty. Be prompt."

And then he spots Charlie pumping up his mother's inflatable reindeer. My former friend does it with such a lack of enthusiasm, it's obvious it will take him all night.

"Put your back into it, boy!" yells Mr. H. "The judges are coming in the morning!"

Charlie's house is the only one that hasn't been decorated to death. I feel a little sorry for him. Plus, his mom has taken on a second shift at the hospital.

That night, after playing waiter and handing out paper cups filled with Mr. H's mulled wine (nonalcoholic), I get out my camera. Everyone is here—everyone except Charlie. Harassed Mother's kids are still wearing their Sunday school nativity play costumes: old dish towels, grubby wings, and badly fitting crowns. Smelly Vincent's baby Jesus costume is covered in a cocktail of boogers and orange juice. Gnome Lady is modeling a tacky red sweatshirt with an embossed Christmas tree that lights up and flashes at two-second

intervals. My mom and dad have put on brightly col-
ored paper birthday hats found in one of the junk
drawers. Charlie's mom arrives late, out of breath,
still in her nurse's uniform. She guzzles down a large
mouthful of "wine" and asks for another.

Mr. H has covered his prized bush with a couple
of large white sheets and has hauled it into the middle of the cul-de-sac. After a Cape Canaveral–style
countdown, he whips them off. My camera captures
the looks on everyone's faces. Disbelief, awe, and
poorly masked horror.

Out of his prized bush, Hedge Man has sculpted a
larger-than-life topiary Santa Claus. In the stunned
silence that follows, Charlie's voice can be heard
clearly from his bedroom window.

"You've got to be kidding."

Okay, it's not really my thing either, but you have
to admire the effort General Xmas has put into it.

"Elf One, illuminate!"

I hit the switch. Smelly Vincent bursts into tears.

If it were just a bush carved into the shape of
Santa, it wouldn't be so bad. But Mr. H, in his blind
ambition to win first place, has taken topiary to the
fourth dimension. A network of LED lights outlines a
giant grinning face. A white flashing beard cascades

over a twinkling red suit. Santa's belt is a running message in lights that reads "MERRY XMAS FROM MORNINGVALE CIRCLE."

"Ladies and gentlemen," Mr. H announces, "I give you our secret weapon. Unfortunately the judges won't be seeing it in its full glory, since their schedule's tight and we got a morning slot. But I think you'll all agree, they're going to be impressed."

It's grotesque, it's horrendous, it's way beyond tacky. It's fantastic.

"Wow," says my mom.

"Ingenious," says Gnome Lady.

"Is there any more wine?" asks Charlie's mom.

But Mr. H is oblivious. His glasses reflect a million tiny lights as he stands, spellbound by the genius of his own creation.

It's past eleven when I hear strange noises coming from outside. I can see from my window that Charlie is still out there trying to inflate his mother's plastic reindeer. I put on my bathrobe over my pj's and go out.

"Looks like you have an inner trig problem. . . ." I smile at him. He doesn't smile back. "Look, I'm really sorry about the way things turned out, but it was kinda dumb to eat the cookies."

"I didn't take the cookies, you idiot. It must have been your crazy sister. You know, you've really changed. 'Elf One! Bring me the fertilizer, Elf One. Sweep up those leaves. Elf One . . . act like a dog. Woof, woof.' When you first moved here, I thought you were cool, but I was wrong. You're just sad."

"Just make sure you get your stupid reindeer blown up," I say. "We think we can win this thing, and you don't want to ruin it for everyone, do you?"

Charlie looks over; drops the limp, half-inflated reindeer; stomps up to me; and sticks his face right into mine. "*I . . . don't . . . care.*" With each word, he punches me in the shoulder.

"You asked for it!" I say, and without a second's hesitation, my fist slams into his stomach. The blow is harder than I meant it to be, but I'm tired, I'm angry, and he is being a real jerk.

"Aaaarrgghh!" he growls. "You're going to be sorry!"

He stands up and charges at me. I turn and run. We end up circling Hedge Man's Santa, around and around like cartoon characters. If only I could keep my mouth shut. If only I could stop running and start laughing, it could have turned out okay. But I couldn't.

"You can't even catch me, you're such a loser," I yell.

Charlie's face becomes unrecognizable with rage. His eyes bulge and his face turns bright red.

"Aaaarrgghh!" he shouts.

He lunges forward, finding new speed and strength. He grabs me by the neck and we both start to go down. At first, the topiary Santa breaks our fall, but then the three of us crash to the ground, dragging down leaves, legs, lights, arms, branches, and miles and miles of electrical wire.

"Oh no," says Charlie.

"Oh no," I say.

Santa lies on his back, only he doesn't look like Santa anymore. He just looks like a small bush covered in junk. His head has been snapped clean off.

"We are in so much trouble," I say.

"Oh no," says Charlie again.

It's early morning, and I've been wide awake all night, worrying about what Hedge Man is going to do to me. This time it wasn't even Elizabeth's fault. It was all mine.

"There's no business like snow business . . ."

For a moment I think I'm dreaming. I even pinch myself to make sure I'm awake. Hedge Man is singing. I leap out of bed and look out the window. The whole world is white. It must have been snowing for hours. Right in the middle of the cul-de-sac, the Santa, in all his illuminated, flashing splendor, beams up at me. Charlie's standing in his driveway, staring in amazement. Two seconds later, I'm down beside him.

"How did you do it?" I whisper to Charlie.

"I didn't do anything," he whispers back. "That's weird . . ."

"What?" I ask.

"I just thought I saw a face, but now it's gone," says Charlie, squinting hard.

"Elf One, Elf Two!" We automatically stand to attention.

"Grab a couple of shovels and start digging! The judges will be here in two hours. We need to get this sidewalk cleared."

"Right away, General X," we both reply.

Later, after the judges are gone and everyone is milling around, congratulating one another on their tremendous effort, I hear a rustle coming from below Santa's sack.

"Hey! Get me a bagel, Frank. I'm starving."

"Elizabeth?"

"Who else would stand in the freezing cold

holding up a Santa head all day?" she says. "You owe me big-time."

The head of Mr. H's topiary Santa mysteriously falls off around lunchtime. But by then it doesn't matter; we've already won first prize.

"Why don't we all chip in and buy the biggest Christmas tree you've ever seen to put in its place?" I say.

"My, you're full of good ideas," Gnome Lady says, putting her arm around me. "I like that in a neighbor."

Hi,
If you are
ever in the
neighborhood,
why not
drop by?
Signed,
Elizabeth
44 Morningvale Cir

Chapter Nine

It's the middle of January and all our Christmas trees are dead and waiting to be hauled away to the wood chipper. A band of teenagers comes in a rusty pickup truck and goes from door to door offering to take them away for two bucks each.

I can hardly believe my eyes. It's Grim Reaper Number Two from last Halloween—minus the cheap black hood, the white makeup, and the black eyeliner. Of course, that's not to say he looks any better. He still has the kind of face that would give you nightmares.

"Aren't you the Grim Reaper?"

"From Halloween? What about it?"

"I just didn't think we'd see you around this neighborhood again."

"You want your tree taken or not?"

"Why are you so nasty?" Elizabeth asks when he's taken our old tree and a couple of dollars. "I heard he's actually kind of nice. Once you get to know him."

"Yeah, I guess he just hangs out with the wrong crowd . . . the undead."

A couple of days later, he's back again.

"Looking for more trees? You'll have to wait till next year," I say.

"I got a note in my locker," he mumbles from behind his long, greasy hair. "It said to drop by this address some time. It's signed 'Elizabeth.'"

"That's my sister."

He stands there and nods for a moment or two and stares out into the distance. Then with a heave, he shoves both hands in the pockets of his low-slung jeans and looks momentarily decisive, in a wimpy kind of way.

"Well . . . uh . . . is she here? Can I, like, see her?"

I can't resist it.

"No," I say, "not exactly."

"Oh." He looks confused.

He obviously hasn't met Elizabeth or he'd get it. On the other hand, he does look pretty dim.

"Elizabeth! Someone is here for you. An agent of death."

From upstairs, we both hear her freaking out.

The Grim One frowns at me. I suspect that this is going to be even better than the time at Halloween when he dropped all the bags and ran away. Elizabeth comes bounding down the stairs.

"Hi," she says softly.

"I'll leave you two alone then," I offer.

His face changes from "hip emo dude who couldn't really care less" to "freaked out" in under a second.

"Wait," says the Reaper. "I didn't realize it was *that* Elizabeth. She's the, she's the, the, the . . ."

As he struggles with one of the shorter words in the English language, only a few seconds pass. But to him it must feel like forever.

"The invisible girl," says Elizabeth flatly. "If you want to be politically correct, you can say 'visibly challenged.'"

Grim Boy's eyes dart from side to side as if he'd be able to see her if only he tried hard enough.

"Whoa, too freaky for me," he mutters. "I'm outta here." And with one last greasy glance in our direction, the Grim One lopes back down the road.

"Eww," I say. "You don't seriously like him, do you? Did you really send him a note?"

But Elizabeth's not listening.

"I can't believe he called me a freak," she says in a quiet voice. "He doesn't even like me. I'm so embarrassed." She thumps back up the stairs.

"Why do you care?" I call up after her. "He's a total loser."

"I hate this town and everybody in it!"

"Calm down, Elizabeth," I say, running up the stairs after her. "What can I do to make you feel better?"

"Start packing."

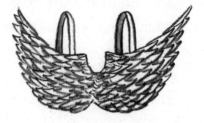

Chapter Ten

It's been about a week now since Elizabeth started her full-on sulk. As I said, no one does it better. It's like sharing a house with a malevolent poltergeist. Doors slam unexpectedly, plates smash, and faucets are left on full blast in the middle of the night. Once she hit me in the face with a cushion for no reason while I was watching TV and nearly gave me a heart attack. Bob's been under my bed since Tuesday. He'll only come out to eat or to go for walks with me. I've taken him on twenty-six already. Plus, Elizabeth really did pack all of her stuff and is now living out of her suitcase. The only thing she stuck with is her radio show, playing one gloomy song after another.

Charlie says that the Grim One broke her heart. He thinks maybe she might need a boyfriend.

"Fat chance that's going to happen. And anyway, she's not old enough for a boyfriend," I say as we stand, shivering, next to the garage so we're out of earshot. "Besides, who'd put up with someone like her?"

As if to illustrate my point, her Boys-R-Us alarm clock comes flying out of the upstairs window and smashes on the sidewalk in front of us.

"Maniac!" I shout. "You almost hit us!"

"Gee whiz, she must be really mad," says Charlie. "That's official tour merchandise."

Mom and Dad are doing the usual, pretending that nothing's wrong. But Dad did ask me the other day what I thought of Pittsburgh. Thank goodness Mom just got some swanky Valentine's Day gig at the town hall. It's the biggest job she's had since we moved here. She wants her waiters and waitresses to dress up as Cupids, with bows, arrows, the works. She's already hit every dollar store and bought all the red paper to make valentine bunting. Plus, she's ordered several crates of pink champagne and a truckload of oysters. I think it all sounds totally gross, but I'm keeping my mouth shut.

Of course, the whole family has been roped into helping her. I was told to cut out five hundred red paper hearts in varying sizes, which she intends to hang from the ceiling. Dad's gluing feathers to huge cardboard wings. Elizabeth has been put in charge of cupcake production.

"Oh . . . ," says my mother. "Aren't they a little bit . . ."

Instead of the pale pink Mom specified, the cakes are a deep, dark, murderous red, the color of congealing blood. Elizabeth must have used an entire bottle of red food coloring in the cake batter.

". . . dark?" says Elizabeth.

"I'm sure they'll be fine," says Mom cheerfully. "We'll slap on some frosting, a little bit of edible glitter, and no one will be any the wiser."

"Oh Mom, come on," I blurt out. "I wouldn't eat one of those if I were starving to death."

"Frank!" she shouts at me. "You have work to do. I need those hearts yesterday."

I go back to my pile of paper hearts. Every single one has been torn in half.

Dad's pulling all the feathers out of an old pillow.

The white fluff is sticking to his eyebrows, his upper lip, his hair. He looks about a thousand years old.

"Son," he says, "get thee to the kitchen and bringeth me back a flagon of hot tea." Mom finds him funny, but I'm still too mad.

"If you see Elizabeth," I say, "tell her I'm going to kill her."

"Frank," says Dad, "we don't use that kind of language in this house. Are you nearly finished with the heart job? I need some help here."

Great. She trashes all my hard work, and I get into trouble. It's the story of my life. But this is not the time to make a fuss. This is not the time to blow the whistle. Even last year I would have gone mental. But I know that this party is really important for Mom. This party is really important for all of us. And if it doesn't go well and Elizabeth gets her way, who knows where we could end up? In another moving van, heading to another life. I pick up my scissors and start cutting again.

When Charlie drops by five hours later, I'm still at it.

"You know that guy who works at Comic Cave?" asks Charlie. "He knows almost every single male between the ages of nine and forty-five. *Single* males."

"So?" I reply.

"Don't you get it? *Single* males!" He's shouting now.

"You mean every single loser, geek, and nerd head?" I say.

"What? That's our favorite shop."

"What's your point, Charlie?"

"Look, Elizabeth needs a boyfriend."

"Not that kind of boyfriend."

"Frank, the Grim Reaper wouldn't even take her! Comic Cave Guy is coming up with a list of the truly desperate."

"Charlie," I say, "that is the stupidest idea you've ever had. Elizabeth will never go for it."

"Well, Comic Cave Guy is already on it. I even traded him *Iron Mask*, Number ten and *Spider Aztec Sting*, Number six, Volume two."

"Hey, those are mine! Whatever your evil plan might be, I can tell you right now, it's a waste of time."

"Just hear me out. . . . We get them together at your mom's Valentine's Day party, they fall in love, and bingo, she's off your back. Simple."

"The only thing around here that's simple is you."

Charlie sticks out his tongue at me and crosses his eyes.

"Charlie, Frank," shouts Mom, "come in here for a second. I need you to try on your waiter outfits."

"What waiter outfit?" asks Charlie.

"It has nothing to do with me," I reply.

Later, I'm lying in bed wide awake even though it's the middle of the night. My hand is killing me from all the cutting, and I can't fall asleep. I'm having visions of more public humiliation as Charlie and I walk around the town hall in our idiotic Cupid getups. Mom said she was short-staffed. I said she was out of her mind. Mom said twenty dollars. Each. Charlie said why not. I suggested plenty of reasons in the "not" camp.

"For twenty dollars," said Charlie, "I'd dress up as Britney Spears."

I laughed so hard it hurt.

"But for that price I'll expect you to be on your best behavior," said Mom.

And so I agreed to the deal. Even though I'm still not convinced it's worth the money.

Dad is way behind on his wings assembly, and Mom is staying up late to give him a hand. I open my bedroom door to go and get a drink of water. It is then that I overhear them talking.

"This one's make or break," says Dad. "What do you think?"

"I think I don't really want to talk about this right now," Mom says.

"But when else can we talk about it? This is serious."

For a second, neither of them says anything.

"You haven't told anybody, have you?" asks Dad.

"Of course not. Okay . . . but if it goes horribly wrong, how about leaving in the middle of the night?" Mom says.

"Yes, that's perfect. That's it," says Dad.

"And then nobody will know."

"See, I told you it wouldn't take long to figure out."

I stand stock-still. This must be a dream. I pinch myself hard. "Ouch!"

"Frank, is that you?" says Mom.

I creep back into my room and gently close the door. My mind starts to race. This party is more important than I realized. Ever since Dad got suspended from the newspaper for reviewing a restaurant that had closed down, Mom's had to shoulder all the pressure. Not to mention my sister's current mood. But things must be much worse than I'd thought; we might have to leave in the middle of the night! If we have to move again, then everything I've worked so hard for will count for nothing. Bob looks up at me with his head to one side, as if he's asking me what's wrong.

"Come here, boy," I say. "Whatever happens, we'll always be together."

Bob jumps up on my bed and rests his head on my stomach. Neither of us manages to fall asleep till dawn.

The night of the party finally arrives. The town hall is lit up inside in every shade of pink you can imagine. There's a chocolate fountain, a cocktail bar, and a stage set up for a band. Who knows what kind of romantic garbage they're going to play? I haven't seen Mom for hours. Last time I saw Dad, he was standing on the top rung of a ladder, holding a huge mirror ball. As for Elizabeth, she's keeping a low profile. So far, so good. Maybe, for once, our family won't mess up. Maybe, for once, we'll get it right. But if not . . . I gaze out of the window toward the shopping center and the busy intersection. If I stand on my tiptoes, I can see the corner of my school.

"What do you think of this town?" I ask Charlie.

He shrugs. "It's a dump," he says.

"Well, I sort of like it," I say.

He looks at me as if I'm crazy.

"You're such a freak sometimes," he says, looking over my shoulder at the traffic heading toward the multistory parking lot or the municipal recycling center.

"I wasn't the one who said he wanted to dress up as Britney Spears."

"That's not what I said," he replies.

"Was too!" I retaliate.

"Boys!" shouts Mom, suddenly appearing with a giant heart-shaped meringue cake covered with pink cream and strawberries. "Have you seen the packet of birthday candles anywhere?"

"Whose birthday is it?" asks Charlie.

"It's the mayor's," she says. "What a sweetheart he is. This cake is a surprise though, so don't say anything. His mother made it. She's lovely too. And guess what? One day, when she was just a girl, she suddenly developed *Formus Disappearus*."

"You mean she's invisible too?" asks Charlie.

"Visibly challenged," says Mom. "Yes. Nobody knows why, but it was just after she met the mayor's father for the first time. Anyway, she's quite a fixture in this town. She makes cakes for almost every birthday, wedding, or anniversary. I have to find those candles . . . I think it's time to get changed into your outfits. And then can you start polishing the—"

Thankfully, her phone rings.

"I don't believe what you are telling me!" she shouts into the mouthpiece. "You know I ordered the scarlet, not the crimson! Hello? Hello?"

Before she rushes out with her phone glued to her ear in search of better reception, she turns to us.

"The silver . . . it's in the plastic crate next to the sink."

"Are we going to get paid extra for that?" Charlie asks me as we examine our Cupid outfits.

"She's probably going to pay us in congealed-blood cupcakes," I say as I pull on my wings. "Who else is going to eat them?"

Charlie looks puzzled. "I snuck one of those earlier . . . they're really good."

"Elizabeth made them. You have to be blind to like those."

"Speaking of which," says Charlie, "I did it. I set it up."

"What are you talking about?"

"The blind date. I set it up," he says. "For your sister."

"What?"

I turn so quickly, my wings knock over an empty cake stand.

"Frank!" shouts Mom from the other side of the hall. "All breakages come out of your pay."

"Yeah, his name is Owen. He's into *Star Trek*. He can even speak a little Klingon. Comic Cave Guy says he's not half bad, other than a very annoying laugh. If she can't snag him, then—"

"Then what?" says my sister.

"Elizabeth," I say.

"Did I just hear you say you set me up on a blind date?" she asks.

"No. Yes. Maybe," says Charlie.

"It wasn't my idea. It has nothing to do with me," I say, as if that will make any difference.

For a second my sister is silent, but it's a furious kind of silence. Her face, if you could see it, would be turning red right now. Her ears, if you could see them, would have steam blowing out of them.

"Frank Black," she seethes, "how do you always manage to spoil my day?"

Maybe it's the outfit or the sleepless night or

maybe even the effect of all the food coloring in Elizabeth's cupcakes—Yeah, I snuck one too—but suddenly I feel a surge of fury coming on like a tidal wave and there's nothing I can do to stop it.

"Spoil *your* day?" I yell. "You've been spoiling my *life* since the day I was born. It's your fault we keep having to move. It's your fault Mom and Dad don't have regular jobs. It's your fault I keep having to move away from any friend I ever make. It's your fault I have to come to this stupid party and wear these stupid wings."

For a moment, nobody says anything. Charlie is staring at me with his mouth open.

"You really think that?" asks Elizabeth.

"Are you going to move?" asks Charlie.

"Yes! You always ruin everything, Elizabeth."

"Well then, I have just one thing to say to *you*," says Elizabeth in a quiet sort of voice. "If you don't call off this blind date garbage, I'll spoil this whole party. And I'll make it look as if it were your fault. And you know I can do it."

The red heart decorations rustle in the air above us. On the other side of the hall, a door slams. Elizabeth is gone. Initially, I feel relieved, but then the enormity of what she just said hits me.

"Are you really going to move?" asks Charlie again.

"Right now, it could go either way," I reply. "What were you thinking, Charlie? This could be ten times worse than the Bang and Bolt Routine. You don't know what she's capable of."

"I'm sorry," he says. "I was only trying to help."

"I know." He sounds so pitiful. "You better call the blind date guy and tell him it's off."

"Wait a minute. What will it matter if he comes or not?" says Charlie. "She won't know who he is, and he won't be able to see her. A real *blind* date! Ha, ha!"

"It's not funny, Charlie. Just call him right now."

"I don't think he carries a cell phone. Although he may have one of those communicators they use on the Starship Enterprise." Charlie starts to laugh at his own joke, until he sees me glaring at him. "I guess I could try his home number."

"If my sister ruins this party, life as we know it is over. It would be a disaster."

"Really?" asks Charlie.

"'Fraid so, my friend, 'fraid so," I say.

Mom appears, holding a large platter of miniature red JELL-O Cupids. Each one has been impaled through the heart with a single toothpick. "What do you think, boys? Too much?"

Charlie and I look at each other. "No, Mom, they're great," I say. "This is going to be a party no one will ever forget."

Chapter Eleven

Have you ever felt as if you are the only person in the whole world who is not having a good time? As if the sun is out for everyone else but it's raining on you? Well, that's me right now. I'm standing as instructed, at the main entrance of the town hall, a tray of smoked salmon appetizers in one hand and my homemade Cupid's bow in the other.

I tell you, Charlie and I have been robbed. Twenty dollars is not enough. Even a thousand would never compensate for the humiliation. But for now we seem to be blending into the background. The cheesy decorations, the paper hearts, and the lights make people stop in their tracks. Nobody in this town has ever seen anything like it before. If this party, as Dad said, is make or break for Mom, then so far it's definitely make. I'm beginning to believe it might wipe out everything Mom and Dad said last night. This is the best party Mom has ever thrown by a million miles. The only problem Charlie and I have, apart from the way we look, is the blind date guy.

Hundreds of guests start to pour in, all the women wearing, well, you can guess what color, and all the men looking like penguins. The mayor's son is here and he's brought tons of friends. Some of them are only a few years older than me. I try not to move. Maybe they'll think I'm a prop.

"Like the outfit, Frank," says Mr. Polwarth, my principal. "Can you fly too?"

"I wish," I reply.

And then he spots the food. "Don't mind if I do," he says and takes four.

Charlie appears, laden down with a vast tray of tiny cheese tarts.

"Any luck calling the blind date guy?" I ask.

"Well, no, not exactly. His mom said he'd already left."

"Oh great," I reply. "You think he's here?"

"How should I know?" says Charlie. "We could try listening for an annoying laugh."

We listen for a minute or two.

"There's a ton of laughing," I say. "And most of it is annoying."

"I'm so sorry. I know this is all my fault," says Charlie. "It was stupid, but I was just trying to help."

"It'll be fine," I reply, trying to make him feel better. "I mean, don't you think a couple of winged waiters can take on a nerd and an invisible girl? We could appetizer them to death."

We both start to smile, and in seconds we're laughing so hard that we can hardly stand up.

"Is that . . . salmon?" some lady says and takes about a dozen in a napkin.

"Take one," I say, trying not to laugh. "Or six."

She looks at me with a frown, as if she's wondering whether or not to report me.

"They're delicious," I add. "Why not eat them while they're hot?"

"Are they hot?" asks Charlie when she's gone.

"No," I reply.

And we both start to laugh all over again.

"I'm glad you're here," I say.

Even though Charlie looks pretty dorky dressed up in the wings and everything, I realize he's the best friend I've ever had. In fact, Morningvale Circle is probably the best place, with the best people, that I've ever lived. And to think, by the time Smelly Vincent stops being smelly, I may be long gone. I like it here. I just don't understand why Elizabeth would want to leave all this behind.

"We'd better unload some of this food before Mom sees us," I say.

"See you later, and don't panic," says Charlie before he disappears into the crowd.

All I can hope for now is that I bump into the blind date guy before Elizabeth does. I start to search the place systematically for a single, lonely *Star Trek* fan.

"Salmon bites anyone?" I say. "Any more salmon bites?"

And then the cheesy music stops and a crackly voice comes over the loudspeaker. The mayor himself is onstage.

"Welcome. I hope you're having a great time," he shouts into a microphone. "Will the owner of the blue Ford Fiesta please return to the vehicle? You're blocking the fire exit. And there's no discount on parking tickets for guests, even if it *is* my birthday!"

The crowd chuckles politely.

"Also, I have a guy up here looking for an Elizabeth. He says he's her blind date and that he'll be waiting for her at the chocolate fountain. Boy, I'll tell you, romance is really in the air tonight."

In the brief space before the music starts up again, a truly horrific laugh booms out from the loudspeakers. It's like nothing I've ever heard before. It doesn't even sound human.

I scan the crowd and lock eyes with Charlie. In military style, I signal for him to man the fountain. I have to move quickly to stop Elizabeth before she does something I can't fix. At the cocktail bar, there's no one except the principal with a glass in each hand. The buffet is packed, three people deep, but it all looks normal. The coatroom looks fine too, with all the coats behaving as coats should. And on the stage, the mayor is sitting on a mock throne that Mom made from a chair she found in a thrift store. Everything is normal—too normal.

Suddenly all the lights dim. A feeling of pure horror envelops me. At the back of the hall, an enormous pink meringue, the one that my mother decorated with candles and glitter, has just appeared. All the candles are burning, but it's floating in midair. Without warning, it starts to bob along at head height, and I realize with a shudder that it's heading toward the stage.

Some people move out of the way when they see me coming, but most people just stand there. By the time I reach it, the cake is only a few feet away from the stage. A familiar song starts to play, but I can't quite place it. I see my mother put her arm around the mayor. They have no idea what's coming.

"Noooooooooooooooooooooo!" I cry as I dive for my sister's legs.

"Aaaarrgghh!" screams a voice from above.

Only it's not my sister. It's an older woman, an invisible older woman, her legs in nylon stockings and her feet in sensible shoes. And I realize with sudden, hideous clarity that I've just floored the mayor's mother. The meringue, her meringue, the meringue she's made specially for her son's birthday, flies up in the air, flips twice, and slowly starts its descent. As everyone watches the cake in freefall, I suddenly recognize the song that's been playing the whole time. Of course, it's "Happy Birthday."

I'm spending some quality time with myself in the parking lot. I am now the loser kid who shoves senior citizens to the ground and ruins birthday surprises. The cake went everywhere: on the walls, on the guests, and, of course, on the mayor. He was so covered in cream that he looked like a pink version of the Abominable Snowman. Although everyone wanted to call for an ambulance, luckily the mayor's mother wasn't injured. She was more upset about her cake.

"Fifteen egg whites," she kept repeating. "Fifteen egg whites, without a hint of yolk . . ."

I see Charlie coming out to look for me and I duck behind a car.

"Are you hiding from me?" he shouts. "Because if you are, you should think about taking off your wings. I can see you a mile away."

"No," I reply. "I was just tying my shoelace."

"Listen, it could have happened to anybody," says Charlie.

"Yeah right."

"It was an easy mistake to make. And guess what? I found the blind date guy. He had so much chocolate from the fountain that he felt sick and had to go home. So everything's going to be okay, right?"

I don't respond. You have to admire the guy; he just doesn't give up.

"Your dad looks really cool tonight," he says. "You should have told me."

"I don't know what you're talking about. Could you just leave me alone now, please?"

Charlie's mouth drops open. "Why are you being so mean? I thought we were friends."

"Not for much longer," I say under my breath. Charlie overhears me and turns and walks away. It's for the best in the long run. When we leave here, at least he won't like me enough to miss me.

If this party is make or break, then it's definitely break. And ironically, Elizabeth had nothing to do with it. I broke it single-handedly. I wonder how long we'll stay here. A week or a couple more days . . . maybe we'll pack up and leave tonight just like Dad said.

The back door of the town hall flies open and a laughing couple comes out for a breath of fresh air. It's the principal and some lady. He spots me.

"Hey, look! A fallen angel in the parking lot," he says.

The lady laughs and sways slightly. I pull off my wings and stuff them under my arm.

"What's wrong, Frank? Don't tell me you're embarrassed to see your dad play? I wish I looked that good in a pair of plastic pants. What a fantastic party!"

Oh, great! The Spits are playing. First I trash the party and now Dad's going to put the final nail in the coffin. I say good-bye, turn to head home, and trip on the curb.

"Where are you going?" asks Elizabeth. "Are you crying?"

"Where have you *been*?" I yell. I can feel the tears streaming down my face, even though I'm trying my best to hold them in.

"I've been around. Why?"

"You missed everything. Did you know we're moving again? Tonight! It's all been arranged."

"What? What are you talking about?"

How can I explain? How can I tell her I was so scared she was going to ruin everything that I was the one who messed up big-time. Maybe I should start with what I heard our parents saying the night before.

"Dad said this one was make or break," I tell her.

As Mr. Polwarth heads back in and the door swings open, the sound of Dad's band comes blasting out from inside the hall.

"*This one's make or break, baby,*" he croons. "*Make or break my heart.*"

They're sounding typically atrocious. I try to ignore them.

"And he said if the party didn't work out, we'd have to leave in the middle of the night."

"We're not going anywhere, Frank."

"But isn't that what you want? To move again?"

"Moving isn't high on my agenda right now."

"But what about the suitcase?"

"I just did that to freak you out."

The next song starts. *"How about leaving in the middle of the night, I know it's crazy but it feels just right."*

"What did he just sing in there?" I ask Elizabeth.

"They have a whole new set of songs," she says. "Don't tell Dad I said so, but they all stink. Still, everyone's loving the party. Mom has another ten bookings already."

Suddenly I realize I have everything wrong. What I was hearing was Dad working out his set list for the band. I must look shocked. I must look overemotional. I am.

"You look like you need a hug, little brother," says my sister.

I reach out for her and find her, amazingly enough. And then she gives me the biggest hug ever.

"I thought I'd lost everything," I say. "My friend, my life, my house."

"Enough," she says, letting me go again. "The only thing you've lost is your mind."

"In this case," I admit, "I have to agree with you."

"Frank," she whispers. "Can you keep a secret? I met this guy. He's really cute. And you'll never guess what—he's the mayor's son. . . ."

Elizabeth chats away, but I'm not really listening. All of a sudden my life seems to have fallen into place: Mom's party is the talk of the town, Dad's band seems to be really rocking, and for once even my sister is happy.

". . . His grandmother has FD," she's saying. "So it doesn't bother him at all. He thinks it's kinda cool. And he's been listening to my school radio show for months. He says he's a huge fan. Can you believe it?"

I spot a pair of wings heading toward the bus stop.

"Hey, wait up!" I yell.

Charlie stops a few feet away but won't look me in the eye.

". . . He has some great playlist suggestions. He's going to e-mail me some links."

"Do you have change for the bus?" Charlie asks.

"It was all a mistake," I say. "I thought because

I'd ruined the party, we'd have to move again. But it was all just Dad's crummy song titles."

As if on cue, the door opens again and another blast of Dad's band's song comes out.

"*Nobody will know*," he sings. "*Oh nobody will know, oh nobody will know, how much I love you, now that you're dead . . .*"

"Cool track," says Charlie. "I think they're sounding pretty good."

"You think so? Really?"

Charlie and I both start to laugh.

"Want to take the bus home?" he says. "We just missed the 46 but the 27 is due in . . ."

He stops midsentence and stares at the spot where Elizabeth is standing.

"He's tall but not too tall," she is saying. "We've read all the same books and both *love* vampire movies. I'm not sure if I should play hard to get and make him wait, or if I should just go out with him on Tuesday. . . . What? What it is?"

In the dim glow of the streetlight, something incredible happens. With a shimmer, like a flash of sunlight streaming through the trees or the flicker of Christmas lights on the snow, my sister suddenly appears. And just as suddenly, she disappears again.

"What are you staring at?" she asks.

"Frank," says Charlie, "she looks just like you."

"Will you stop it," she says. "You're scaring me."

"Elizabeth," I say, "we both just saw you. . . ."

"That's impossible," she says. "Isn't it?"